Please renew/return this item by the last date shown.

So that your telephone call is charged at local rate, please call the numbers as set out below:

	From Area codes 01923 or 0208:	From the rest of Herts:
Renewals:	01923 471373	01438 737373
Enquiries:	01923 471333	01438 737333
Minicom:	01923 471599	01438 737599

L32b

LEOPARD IN THE FOLD

'She's a leopard in the fold, God knows whose throat she'll tear out. Maybe Dave's.'

Storm has just married Dave Morley, but their affair had begun before her husband's death and it is this that arouses the enmity of Hector Morley who also fears that Storm will disrupt the very close-knit unity of the Morley family. In the clash between the patriarchal Hector and this beautiful, vengeful young woman, Storm is prepared to use any means to further her ends, even exploiting the innocence of a child.

The Morleys have wealth, power and influence, but especially after the death of Marie Morley, Hector's wife, who was the real focus of unity and love in the family, will these be enough to fight the 'leopard'?

Leopard in the Fold

A NOVEL BY

Joy Packer

EYRE METHUEN · LONDON

First published 1967 by
Eyre & Spottiswoode (Publishers) Ltd
© *Joy Packer 1967, 1969*
Reprinted 1977 and 1979 by Eyre Methuen Ltd
11 New Fetter Lane, London EC4P 4EE
Printed in Great Britain
by Whitstable Litho Ltd, Whitstable, Kent

ISBN 0 413 44440 6

AUTHOR'S NOTE

All the characters and situations
in this novel are
entirely fictitious.

Cape Peninsula   JOY PACKER

CONTENTS

I

DAVE

Mrs Morley looked up at her eldest son, Kevin, and saw his large myopic brown eyes flash behind his spectacles. His narrow beaky nose seemed to grow more pinched and he flexed his long fingers in a helpless gesture.

'What's your brother been up to?' she persisted. 'Gambling, women?'

She was small and birdlike and, in common with many small women, more forceful than she appeared. Kevin shrugged his broad shoulders and prepared for an inquisition. If she wanted the answers she'd get them sooner or later so he might just as well make it easy for both of them.

'One notorious woman,' he said. 'And a scandal that's set all Johannesburg by the ears.'

His mother studied him, her eyebrows arched. So this was the reason why Kevin had brought his wife, Colleen, and their four-year-old son, Hudson, from Johannesburg to the Cape to spend an unexpected fortnight with his parents.

'The moment I saw you and Colleen at the airport this morning I knew something was wrong. I guessed immediately that you'd come all this way to break unpleasant news to us.' Mrs Morley prided herself on her intuition.

Kevin grinned and his whole face grew younger. He patted his mother's narrow delicate hand.

'All is not yet lost, Mum. We came for other reasons too. There's tremendous expansion going on here in Somerset West and we're going to open a Real Estate agency here – a branch of our Johannesburg firm.'

'What's that, my boy?'

Kevin turned his head quickly towards the open door-way where his father paused with the two golden labradors, Amber and Topaz, at his heels. The Old Man was an imposing figure, an erect sinewy six foot three of well preserved muscle and bone, a thatch of grizzled hair, aquiline features and a dominating air of confident purpose. All his life he had been very much the head of his family, indulgent with his children up to a point, though unhesitating in making the vital decisions that would influence the course of their lives, but even so his wife could usually lead him by that arrogant nose. Well, she wouldn't find it easy this time, thought Kevin. She'd always placed herself as a gentle buffer between her husband's wrath and her children's misde-meanours, but now even she would be hard put to it to intervene on her son's behalf. The Old Man would never tolerate a first class scandal.

Hector shot an enquiring glance at his wife and son, who were standing in front of a glowing fire, for the spring day was bright but cold. The long room was beautifully propor-tioned and furnished as was the rest of Blue Horizon, the Somerset West mansion Hector Morley had bought at the Cape after the miraculous discovery of a rich vein of gold on his farm, Blue Horizon, in the Transvaal. Both the home of his working years and that of his retirement had been well named. The original Blue Horizon at the northern limit of the Reef had looked out towards far smoke coloured ridges under the ever shifting violet of cloud shadows and the haze of blue distance that shrouded the limitless veld. Here, at the Cape, it was a more intimate horizon and a more vivid blue. The wide lawn and lavish rose-garden in front of the house were backed by a jacaranda grove that in spring was a mass of ethereal hyacinth blossom; beyond it glittered the cobalt curve of False Bay held between the lavender horns of the Simonstown and Hottentots-Holland mountains.

As the Old Man advanced into the room with his dogs he could see his wife twice over, the small dainty figure in front of the hearth and the portrait above it. The portrait had been painted by a famous artist five years earlier when Hector had just acquired his fortune. The artist had caught the essence of his subject, her intense femininity, the large melting brown eyes that held such sparkling gaiety combined with a subtle suggestion of authority, the neat small features and the sensuous appealing mouth. Marie Morley's was a face no man would find it easy to resist. It was curiously Latin with the greying dark hair, the warm olive skin and the eyes inherited from her Huguenot ancestors. It was a fine portrait of the mistress of her home and of her husband, Hector often thought with amusement. It's more austere twin, the portrait of the master of Blue Horizon and his family, brooded over the large dining-room.

When Hector had received his first share in the new gold-field he had made a generous Trust for his three sons, Kevin, Dave and Franz, and his daughter, Magda, and then he had taken his wife and his daughter for a world cruise. On their return Hector and Marie had moved into their new home where the modest home-farm kept Hector busy and happy.

Kevin was already married by then and living in Johannesburg, where he directed a thriving Real Estate firm. Dave
was at Witwatersrand University, Franz was still at school,
and before long there was a wedding at Blue Horizon for
Magda and Jules Strauss, a promising young general practi-
tioner in Cape Town. Now, four years later, Dave was in
business with Kevin, and Franz was studying agriculture in
California. The only cloud over the family contentment was
the fact that Magda, who longed for children, was still
childless.

'Did I understand you to say you were going to open a
branch of Morley Bros. here in Somerset West?' asked
Hector Morley.

'Yes, Dad. I've come down specially to see about it. There
is great development going on in these parts. Can I give you
a sherry?'

'What are you drinking yourself, Kev? Gin and tonic?
Yes. That'll do me. No lemon.'

The Old Man took the glass from his son. 'A Somerset
West branch is a good idea, but isn't it rather a sudden
decision?'

Kevin smiled. 'Perhaps. But it occurs to me that the
branch will serve two purposes. It'll pay us hands down and
it'll get Dave out of harm's way. I'll put him in as manager.'

The Old Man's shaggy eyebrows shot up.

'Out of harm's way? I don't understand.'

His wife intercepted quietly.

'There's a woman in Dave's life – as usual. Someone
rather unsuitable, I gather. You'd better tell us everything,
Kev.'

Kevin said, 'Well, if I don't, someone else will. So here

goes. He's hopelessly tied up with Storm Barralet, the wife of old Sidney Barralet, the financier. She's about Dave's age, round twenty-four. She has a daughter of five – a little girl called Gabrielle – and rumour has it that she's cruel with the child. At all events, Storm and Dave have been inseparable for weeks now.'

'He's subject to infatuations,' sighed his mother. 'And he likes exotic women. But he gets over these attacks in time.'

'I've heard of Sidney Barralet,' said Hector. 'Isn't he in deep waters with his companies?'

'That's right. He was rich as Croesus a few years ago, but now he's old and very sick – heart, I believe – and on the verge of a physical and financial collapse.'

'So his scheming wife would like to get her hands on some Morley money, no doubt,' suggested the Old Man grimly.

'No doubt,' agreed Kevin. 'But Dave's fortune is peanuts to her and you're good for another twenty years at least.'

The Old Man chuckled. 'We live too long these days.' Then his thick brows knitted. 'So Dave's carrying on with a woman whose husband is on his deathbed.'

'And how!' Kevin's wife, Colleen, had joined them with her small son, Hudson. She was slender and pretty with black hair and green eyes and a lively face. The Old Man was fond of her, she was the ideal contrast to her rather taciturn husband.

'What can I get you, my dear? Gin and tonic with lemon? Sherry —'

'Gin and tonic with lemon, please, Dad. So Kev's been telling you about Dave and Storm Barralet?'

'And about the new branch he hopes to open here,'

added Mrs Morley, 'to get our Dave out of this harpy's clutches.'

Her grandson was opening her handbag and examining the contents; she took it from him and offered him a bottle opener instead. She liked the idea of having her son Dave so near – perhaps living in the house with them. He'd get over Storm Barralet once he was out of her way. He was fickle and there were plenty of pretty girls at the Cape to distract him.

'There's certainly room for another Real Estate agency here,' approved Hector, who, like his son Kevin, had a nose for land values and development. 'There'll be new townships springing up in this area soon.'

'That's what I thought, Dad. I'd like to go into the whole thing with you later,' said Kevin. 'There's a lot of new building going on. People settle here. There's quite a colony from Kenya alone, and, like you and Mum, up-country people often choose to retire to the Cape – especially this area. Hallo, here's Mag!'

A young vital brown haired woman with warm grey eyes surged into their midst, embraced her brother and sister-in-law effusively and swamped little Hudson with her welcome, gaily ruffling his black curls.

'Jules couldn't come to lunch,' said Magda. 'He's overworking as usual. And his back's giving him hell, poor darling. It's really too bad, but he just soldiers on. He sends lots of love and he'll see you later.'

She hugged her parents, patted the dogs and took a cigarette box from Hudson who was about to scatter the contents on the carpet.

'Yes, Daddy, you've guessed it. Tomato juice for me.

Come and sit on my lap, Huddie. Look, I have a wooden swizzle stick you can play with. Mum, did you tell Kevin and Colleen about Franz?'

Hudson attempted to ask what a swizzle stick was for, but nobody paid any attention to him. Mrs Morley said:

'Darling, I haven't had time. There's so much news to exchange and they only arrived half an hour ago.'

'What about Franz?' asked Colleen, interested.

'Well, he's met up with some Australians in California,' said Mrs Morley. 'And he's going to Australia with them when they go back. He wants to take a job as a jackaroo on a sheep station.'

'A jackaroo?' said Kevin. 'That's a sort of apprentice, isn't it?'

'Yes, it will be useful experience for him,' put in Hector.

'And who's the girl in the case?' asked Colleen with a knowing flash of her green eyes.

Magda laughed. 'Ah, now! We gather her name is Philippa Collins. Her father has big mining interests in Western Australia. They live in Perth but they have friends all over the country. Mr Collins has fixed up Franz with this jackaroo job in New South Wales – somewhere near a place called Broken Hill.'

'That's a long way from Western Australia according to my elementary geography,' said Kevin. 'Australia's so big it could swallow up South Africa any time. If this girl, Philippa, lives in Perth she won't see much of Franz in Broken Hill. Sounds safe enough to me.'

'Won't she just!' Magda bounced her nephew on her knee in an effort to prevent him from grabbing at her glass of tomato juice. 'Phil Collins works in Broken Hill. She teaches in the School of the Air, whatever that may mean.'

'Black Swan, the sheep station, is some seventy or eighty miles from Broken Hill,' said Mrs Morley complacently. 'She'd hardly be the girl next door at that distance. Anyway Franz is only twenty-two. Give him a chance!'

She rose and pressed a bell and a few moments later an impressive apparition appeared in the doorway dressed in a white linen suit and red sash and announced that lunch was served. This coal black Bantu was Elijah, the butler who had come to the Cape with his master and who disappeared at intervals to spend the hut building season with his family in the Transvaal. There he bought cattle, sowed crops, and made sure that his wife would give him a new son or daughter to welcome him on his next return to his home-land. Meanwhile he worked on fairly amicable terms with old Lettie, the coloured cook, who made allowances for Elijah's fits of temperament as being only natural in the son of a Chief. But although they might work together they did not eat together. Elijah had his food on a tray in his own quarters and he ate more meat and bread than the rest of the household put together. He despised fish or vegetables as was the way of a man born and bred hundreds of miles from the sea in the heart of the grainland.

Kevin smiled as they went in to lunch. 'There's a gambler to beat our Dave. Does Elijah still play the horses?'

The Old Man laughed. 'Luckily for him he has better tipsters than your brother. And gambler or not, he always sends a fair proportion of his wages home. I only wish Dave were half as reliable.'

As they entered the dining-room the Old Man made a sign

to his dogs who immediately sprawled one in each corner
with the portrait of their master between them. Topaz and
Amber knew, like everyone else in Blue Horizon, that here
the Master's slightest gesture was law.

That evening while Kevin discussed the new Somerset
West branch of Morley Bros. with his father, Dave Morley
and Storm Barralet strolled together in the grounds of
Kevin and Colleen's Johannesburg home a thousand miles
away.

Dave had obliged his brother by locking up his bachelor
flat and staying in Kevin's house in the absence of its owners.
'I don't like leaving the place unoccupied – even for a few
days,' Kevin had said. 'There are too many burglaries when
the coast is clear.'

The Spring evening was soft and warm with lightning
playing over the distant horizon. The rains were late and the
thirsty veld was still tawny. The Jersey herd was stabled for
the night, the last sleepy birds twittered in the cypresses
round the swimming pool, and down in the valley clusters
of lights sprang up and blinked their concentrated human
message in the vast landscape. Further to the south the loom
of Johannesburg glowed steadily against the darkening sky.

Storm Barralet slipped her arm through Dave's.

'How dry it smells! Crumbling earth and brittle grass.
Every night the thunderheads build up but the rain holds
off.'

She looked up at Kevin Morley's austere white house with
the burglar scrolls on the plate glass ground floor windows
and a wrought iron balcony above. She had never been here
before. Dave's brother and his wife greeted her coolly when

they met. If they hadn't happened to be away she knew that she would not be in this garden now. But they'd have to accept her one of these days. She'd see to that!

She was aware of a new agreeable intimacy with Dave here. They had walked down to the dam and round the farm buildings in the cool of the evening, they had talked to Geography, the old Bantu dairyman, and to Geometry, his brother, who was the nightwatchman. Of course Geography and Geometry had Bantu names but those were for their personal use and not for the benefit of their white employers. The labradors, Whisky and Sherry, progenitors of Topaz and Amber, had accompanied them, and for once Storm had felt her love affair with Dave to be free of its constricted hothouse atmosphere. We could be friends, she thought surprisingly, yet friendship with a man had never been other than a razor's edge for Storm. She glanced up at his lean face with the sensual mouth contradicting the bony features and he paused in response to the slight pressure of her arm against his. Walking together, dancing together, making love, there was always this physical unity.

'Where do you sleep?' she asked. 'Which is your window?'

'That one on the left with the little balcony outside it. It's the spare-room.'

'I'd like to see it. I'd like to see all over the house. Your brother has quite a set-up here, hasn't he?'

'He was very clever at seeing the way Johannesburg was expanding. All this was wilderness a few years ago when they found gold on Blue Horizon. Dad gave each of us a lump sum then and Kevin spent a good deal of his on buying land here. Now it's trebled its value and is becoming an increasingly important suburb. But you can still run a property like this and a dairy farm, and the Jerseys pay their way handsomely. So do Colleen's Leghorns. Kevin and Colleen have a first-class farm manager, but whenever the family goes on holiday I come and babysit the house like I'm doing now.'

'Nobody leaves a house untenanted these days,' she agreed. 'Are you quite alone here?' His arm tightened on hers.

'Except for Joseph, the cook, who comes from the compound when I need him.'

'Did you tell Joseph I was dining with you tonight?'

They had reached the patio and she flung herself down on a garden chaise-longue. A drink tray had already been set out. He poured her a whisky on-the-rocks.

'Yes – that is if Sidney will spare you.'

He put the glass beside her and offered her a cigarette. As he bent to light it he was aware of the musk and amber of this woman. When she was warm her scent changed its character and sharpened. She raised her eyelids lazily to reveal those slant tawny eyes, cynical now.

'Sidney isn't expecting me back till late. He thinks I'm going to a movie with Rosalind, that dear useful old school chum of mine.'

He grinned. Rosalind – the non-existent stooge, the mythical but essential alibi – never let them down.

They dined on the patio, watching the zig-zag flash of distant storms. Lightning and the roll of thunder excited her.

'The blitz must have been like this,' she said. 'I've always envied my mother, living dangerously through the middle of a war. She conceived my brother in London – in '41 – during the blitz. My father was a South African pilot on leave. Mother was English – and, yes, they were married! They'd been out dancing, some underground joint, and they got back to their hotel with bombs raining down and bursts of A-A fire and the beauty of starshells floating out of the sky criss-crossed with searchlights – a glorious inferno. They didn't go to a shelter, they went to their hotel room and made love, expecting to be blown to bits that way, in the very act of loving. Well, they weren't. My brother, Rodney, was the product of that night. The war ended four years later and I was born into the atomic age. It was a night of storm too – but one of nature's storms. After that my father went on to fight and die in Korea. A good way to die perhaps – in battle – in your prime.'

Dave refilled her glass with the red wine of Constantia. The lights spun gold in her hair and brightened her strange eyes.

'You've never talked much about your parents,' he said.

'They scarcely existed for me. My father was killed when I was five and soon after that my mother – she was always unstable – became an alcoholic. My brother and I were raised by an aunt who loathed us both but did her duty by us, I suppose. Oh, I guess we were probably loathsome and we certainly hated her too. We couldn't wait to grow up and escape – that was how we thought of it – to get away from her and escape. Naturally, Rod was the first to go. He got a job as a motor mechanic. Fast cars were all he cared about. He was killed racing Italian cars in South America. Meanwhile I'd landed myself a job as a model —'

'After that you married Sidney Barralet. For love? For security? For a place in society?'

'Never mind why I married Sidney. I was eighteen. One does stupid things at eighteen. Now I'm the mother of a girl of five, the wife of a man rising sixty —'

'And the mistress of another your own age.'

She gave her throaty laugh. 'Mistress. Lovely word! The girl who cracks the whip!'

The way she said it disquieted him with its hint of domination, even sexual deviation and cruelty. Yet he knew her fierce inflammable passion to be as natural as a wild creature's or he would never have lost himself in this obsessive infatuation that so upset and enraged his brother. Kevin had reduced it to its most material form.

'She wants your money and the fortune she expects you to inherit. Don't pin medals on yourself, Dave! It's not just you she's after. Why do you think she married old Sidney Barralet in the first place?'

Dave had wondered only too often but he sprang to Storm's defence.

'She was a child then and he was a man of the world.'

Kevin's spectacles had flashed as he turned on his brother. 'Child, my foot! Storm was a top model and she was a damn side more than that. She was a beautiful chattel, to be bought and sold. And soon she'll be in the market again. Look out, Dave, or you'll be taken for a ride.'

'Mind your own bloody business!' Dave had said, and for days the brothers had treated one another as enemies.

'You're very quiet,' said Storm, as she poured their coffee. 'What are you thinking about, Dave?'

'You. I'm going to miss you very much.'

'Miss me?'

He took the coffee cup from her – black, no sugar – and

watched her sit down, placing her own cup and saucer carefully beside her. Behind her Joseph was clearing the table. Dave turned and spoke to the Bantu.

'You can go home when you've cleared, Joseph. Leave the coffee tray and I'll put it inside when I lock up.'

'Yes, Baas Dave. Goodnight. Goodnight, Madam.'

'Goodnight, Joseph.' She flung the words over her shoulder. To Dave she repeated:

'Miss me? I don't understand. There isn't any question of your going away, is there?'

The night had turned sultry, the waning moon obscured by heavy rainclouds banked along the horizon. Thunder grumbled and the sheet lightning was nearer now.

'Kevin is opening a branch office near Cape Town. I am being transferred. That's why he's gone down to the Cape. I'll be in charge. It's a step up for the junior partner.'

She said nothing. Down under the cypresses they could see the dark figure of the nightwatchman, Geometry, carrying his heavy knopkierie which could fell a man if wielded with force. The pale shapes of the dogs went with him. Presently Joseph would cross his path on the way home to the Bantu compound where the farm labourers and their families lived in the neat dwellings Kevin had erected for them. In its own simple fashion it was a productive little community with a mealie patch at the back of every home. The compound dogs there were in a different category from the Morley labradors, but every now and again a hint of silky blond crept into the coat of some cur. Hens scratched in modest fowl runs, and radio aerials rose from almost every roof. There was always the music of Radio Bantu to be heard down there – harmonious, monotonous, punctuated

by the resonant voices of the dark announcers. Milk and
butter were supplied to the compound families from
Kevin's dairy and from time to time a beast of the Morley
herd was slaughtered for some special celebration.

Geometry greeted the pair in the patio as he passed that
way in the course of his rounds. He had the dignified
manners natural to his people. Dave exchanged a few re-
marks with him and the older man touched his woollen
headgear as he continued on his tour of his master's property.

'When do they plan to get you out of my clutches?'
Storm asked suddenly as the watchman rounded the side of
the house.

'What do you mean?'

'Exactly what I say. I always do. This transfer. It is
obviously to get you away from me before it's too late.'

'Isn't it too late already?'

She looked thoughtfully into the night where a bat
winged to and fro among the trees.

'I'm not sure,' she said at last. 'Yours is a powerful family
group. They won't let one member out of line if they can
help it. They're like royalty. The marriages have to be
sanctioned by the king and queen.'

'There isn't any question of marriage,' said Dave. His gas
lighter flared as he lit his cigarette and she saw the sudden
tightening of his jaw and the fine strength of his hands.
'You're already a married woman.'

'Mmn. Would it make any difference if I were free?'

'You know it would.'

'Do I?'

He rose, saturnine despite the laughter that rose readily to
his lips and eyes.

'Let's go indoors. You wanted to see over the house.'

'And your sister-in-law, Mrs Kevin Morley, will certainly never invite me here voluntarily. So now's my chance. Is that it?'

'It is. So come.'

An hour later as the crash of thunder shook the house and white lightning flashed over her supine body in a livid glow, Storm turned to Dave and laid her hands over his bare chest.

'Thump, thump. Steady and at peace in spite of the storm outside. It was like making love in the blitz, wasn't it, Dave? Or so I should imagine —'

'Hush!'

He silenced her with his finger upon her soft full lips. The quality of the night had changed. The air was sweet and pure and there was a pattering on the balcony outside the room – light at first, scattered and unsure, and then suddenly strong. A deluge – the end of tension.

'Ah,' he breathed. 'At last – the rain!'

Dora, the Bantu Red Cross night nurse, met her when Storm let herself into her home shortly after midnight.

'Master was tired and went to bed early,' she told Storm in her concise soft-voiced English. 'He was not well.'

'Will Master be awake?'

'I think he will be sleeping. I gave him one of his tablets an hour ago. But it will be necessary to order more from the chemist tomorrow.'

'I'll see to it.' Storm paused and then said suddenly: 'What would happen if you did not give Master his pill when he asks for it?'

'He would feel very sick – with a bad pain in his chest –
a tight pain like an iron band. Tighter, tighter. Many pains.
If he did not get his tablet soon he could not live.' She
pronounced the last word 'leave'. Softly and sadly.

'Then he must always have these tablets near at hand.
Always?'

'Always, Madam.'

'We must be careful.'

'Master is careful himself. He carries them in his pocket.
But he needs the water. It is impossible for him to swallow
them comfortably without water. For some people it is like
that.'

Storm nodded. She turned and went upstairs. Sidney's
room adjoined hers and next to it was the dressing-room
where the night nurse sat with the door ajar between her
and her patient. Storm cleansed off what remained of her
make-up and dabbed cold cream onto her skin. She felt
relaxed and satisfied and she longed to hum a tune – purr it –
as she brushed her shoulder length hair, but Sidney might
wake. She always liked background music in her house –
tape recorded or long playing records.

When she was ready for bed she opened her door and
tiptoed into her husband's room and stood for a long
moment looking down at him. A shaded night-light burned
near his bed and his windows were usually open for he
hungered for air – air that tonight was fresh from the recent
downpour. Deep shadows intensified the skull-like look of
his bald head. Storm knew that Sidney did not fear to die
and tonight he looked near death with his hollow cheeks,
sunken eyes, and blue lips puffing outwards with every
exhalation. She saw his pale clawlike hand clutch at the

sheet and she leaned down and touched his fingers lightly. How cold they were! So old and lifeless compared with the warm urgent hands of the young man who had recently possessed her. She shivered, suddenly afraid of her own thoughts.

As if a nightmare disturbed him, Barralet moaned deeply and suddenly his eyes jerked open and he sat up, staring at his wife. She found herself looking into a face bewildered and bedevilled by some unknown terror.

'You moaned,' she said. 'I thought it might be a bad dream.'

'A cat jumped onto my bed,' he mumbled, still half in sleep. 'It was creeping up towards my face to lie on it and suffocate me.'

She patted his shoulder soothingly. 'Our cat has better things to do on spring nights. There's no cat here. Do you want anything? A glass of water perhaps?'

'Yes – something to rid me of that dream.'

'You have these nightmares often, Sidney?'

'Often enough. I had a slight heart attack tonight. You were late back from the cinema.'

'I went back to Rosalind's flat for coffee. I'm sorry. It wasn't a good show. Actually we left before the end.'

She filled a glass from the iced thermos jug at his bed-side. 'Here you are. Drink this and turn over and sleep again. If you need anything else Dora is next door.'

'Thank you, Storm.'

'That's all right. You're safe now. I'm home.'

She stopped and brushed his forehead with her lips.

''Night Sid. Slaap gerus en droom met lus.'

'I may sleep peacefully but I've had enough dreams for

one night! Even the sweetest couldn't be sweet enough.
Keep them for yourself, honey.'

Storm's laughter whispered softly in her throat as she went
back to her own room.

'I will,' she whispered. 'Droom met lus . . . dream as you
would desire . . . I'll do that . . .'

2

FRANZ

MORLEY BROS. OPENED THEIR LOCAL REAL ESTATE branch in Somerset West early in the New Year with Dave in charge assisted by his capable secretary, Hetty Conradie, an attractive widow in her early thirties, no children and a strongly developed but thwarted maternal instinct which was channelled towards her employer. When she read in the papers shortly after their arrival that Sidney Barralet, Johannesburg financier, had gone insolvent and died soon afterwards of a heart attack, she pointed out the news item to the cousin with whom she lodged.

'Now the sparks are going to fly, Carrie. The Barralet woman's got her hooks into Dave Morley. You mark my words!'

Within the month Dave Morley had flown to Johannesburg, married Storm Barralet by special licence, returned to the Cape with his new wife and little step-daughter, Gabrielle, and faced his family with the *fait accompli*.

Hector Morley and his wife received the newly-weds at Blue Horizon in the company of Magda and Jules Strauss. No congratulations were offered, an excellent dinner was consumed in an arctic atmosphere of impending doom generated by the host, and after Elijah had removed the coffee Hector Morley addressed those few members of his family present upon an occasion which clearly merited condolences rather than celebration. He sat solemnly warming a brandy goblet between his long-fingered hands, his lips thin and his heavy brows scowling over hostile eyes. Even in this dark mood he was an exceptionally handsome man, and, as he well knew, impressive. Mrs Morley watched him anxiously. He would pull no punches tonight although he had promised her to be reasonable. She dared not hope that the tolerance upon which he prided himself would include the young widow who had 'trapped' his son. Magda, her colour heightened by tension, passed a quick glance at Dave's sensitive features set in the mould of obstinate resistance she knew so well. His brandy was untouched at his elbow. Jules Strauss, stiffly seated in a high chair, his back rigid, allowed himself to study the beautiful face of his new sister-in-law. Her oblique golden eyes were wary as she prepared to meet a clash of wills with the head of the family. There was nothing weak about her. She looked dangerous and aggressive, an antagonist worthy of the Old Man's steel.

'We have not met here tonight to welcome Dave's bride into our family,' began Hector frankly. 'The indecent haste of this marriage is an affront to the living and the dead. But, since it has taken place, we, as a family, are compelled to adopt an attitude towards the situation for the sake of convention —'

'Does convention matter so much?' cut in Dave. 'Storm and I had good reasons for our action.'

'That may be,' growled the Old Man in the deep voice that could thunder upon occasion. 'But a wedding held practically at the graveside of the bride's dead husband is something I find almost intolerable. However, at your mother's earnest insistence, Dave, I am prepared to accept Storm in my home, and I hope that Magda and Jules will do the same.'

Jules observed the flash in Storm's eyes and the tightening of her lips. Her hands were clenched on the arm of her chair and he guessed that her long nails drove into her palms.

'I have spoken to Kevin on the telephone,' continued Hector. 'He agrees with me, and Franz will no doubt feel the same when he hears the news. We are a united family and it would be tragic to allow this hasty marriage to disrupt it. Kevin and Dave are business partners, the rest of us live in the same close society within a few miles of one another. So let us at least retain some semblance of unity and dignity in our outward behaviour towards Storm and each other. Dave's wife is a Morley now – no matter what the circumstances – and, as such, my home will be open to her.'

'Perhaps we should tell you the exact circumstances.' Storm's husky voice was low and the left side of her upper lip lifted slightly to show sharp white teeth. 'I am expecting a baby – Dave's, of course – in six month's time. It seemed better to us to have this child – this Morley baby – in wedlock. We could have waited for a conventional period of mourning to elapse, but then the child would have been born Barralet.'

'We preferred to meet the situation as honestly as possible,' added Dave.

Magda sprang to her feet. 'The old blackmail. I'm pregnant, so you must marry me!'

Storm shot back fast. 'Perhaps I was lucky to be able to bring it off.'

She was smiling, but her strange eyes blazed as she stared at Dave's hot-tempered barren sister with a mixture of pity and contempt.

'That'll do!' Mrs Morley's tone was sharp and authoritative. 'I'll have no bickering under my roof. Your father asked you here tonight to establish Storm's position in the family. That has been done. That is all.'

Jules thought: Storm would like to tell the lot of them to go to hell, but she has an eye to the future. She's calculating and, if being accepted as a Morley will pay off in the long run, she'll put up with the Old Man's patronage. And she'll do as they've done all their lives – try to win him over through Mum's influence. Magda says the Old Man has cut Dave out of his will. She won't swallow that easily.

Dave was thinking: She knows the Old Man has cut me out of his will, yet she's prepared to be tolerated by him. She must think she can change his mind, given time. She doesn't know my father! Dave was relieved, though, that she had not forced him to break with his family. The brush with Magda had been a pity but Magda had asked for it. Meanwhile, if everybody kept up the pretence that Storm was as welcome at Blue Horizon as any other Morley, the fiction might in time become a partial fact, though his father, he knew, would never forgive him for the scandal she had caused.

Magda thought: I hate her. She's evil.

When they were alone the Old Man turned to his wife, his brows knitted.

'She's formidable. We might have done better to turn our backs on her entirely.'

'And make an outcast of Dave?'

'She's a leopard in the fold,' he said. 'God knows whose throat she'll tear out. Maybe Dave's.'

Franz Morley heard the news of his brother's marriage in Hawaii. He was on his way from San Francisco to Australia with Mr and Mrs Collins and their daughter, Philippa, and they had broken the long flight to spend four days in Honolulu.

The cable from South Africa awaited him at the hotel on Waikiki Beach. He read it in the privacy of his bedroom. DAVE MARRIED STORM BARRALET IN JOHANNESBURG JANUARY 20 MAGDA.

Franz went out onto the little balcony overlooking the corner of the long shining beach. The sea sparkled in bands of jewel-like colour, sapphire, jade, aquamarine and even ruby far out where the coral reef kept the sharks at bay. Surf-riders and canoe outriggers rode the long breakers, children waded in the shallows, oiled near-nude bodies lay on the sand absorbing the tropical sun, and in a tall date palm outside his window a pair of warblers held a fluted conversation. The hotel garden was shaded by palms, magnolias, baobabs, frangipani and other flowering shrubs. The air was soft and scented and somewhere a guitar twanged gently to the accompaniment of the murmur of the sea. It was mid-morning and Franz had promised to meet Philippa on the beach outside the hotel. But first he drew a letter from his wallet and re-read it. It was from Magda, and he had received it a fortnight ago in California.

'Franz, my dear. What wonderful plans you are cooking. San Francisco, Hawaii, Australia and a job in the outback. I'm jealous. It all sounds so exciting and carefree, and here things are pretty sultry. Dave is besotted with a notorious Johannesburg widow, Storm Barralet. He's been having an affair with her for some time – before her husband died – and Kevin transferred him to the new Somerset West branch to get him out of the way. Well, it hasn't worked. Her husband went broke and had a fatal heart attack just after Dave left Johannesburg. Now Dad has got wind of the affair and threatens to cut Dave out of his will if he persists with his intention of marrying Mrs Barralet whose reputation is evidently hot. Dave won't talk about it but he has got that stubborn look on his face most of the time and I suspect he means to spring her on us in the near future and take a chance on the family reactions . . .'

He refolded the letter and put it back into his wallet with the cable. So Dave had defied the Old Man and the disapproval of the family. He wondered what she was like – this 'notorious widow'. If she was marrying Dave for his money she'd be disappointed. His income was fairly good but nothing like as good as his prospects and those would evaporate if his father carried out his threat to cut him out of his will. The Old Man, moreover, was generous with his children. It pleased him from time to time to give them generous presents when his shares stood high. If Dave was to be denied those cuts off the cake he would hardly be a worthwhile catch for the designing woman Storm Barralet appeared to be.

A light breeze whispered through the bamboo blinds and slatted door as Franz unpacked his suitcase and put on his bathing trunks. There was a bathing towel in the bathroom. He took it and went along the richly carpeted corridor to the bather's elevator and in a few minutes he was on the beach with Philippa.

'Hi, Phil.'

He squatted down beside her as she lay on the warm fine sand – not silver like South African sand, but pale gold.

'Hi, Franz. No bad news, I hope.'

She had seen him collect his cable as they went in to the hotel.

'Depends what you call bad news,' he grinned. 'My brother, Dave, has married a notorious widow – my sister's description – whose husband is scarcely cold in his grave. Not the sort of thing my old man will take kindly.'

She sat up, her bronzed arms round her knees, her dark curly hair glistening in the sun. Her toe-nails were painted coral and her feet were slim and unblemished. She wore no make-up save lipstick. Her skin glowed and a few freckles banded her blunt straight nose. Hers was a gay and laughing face and he loved the turn of her oval jaw, the long neck, the wide shoulders, the tapering hips and legs. Her bikini bra revealed the firm rounded swell of her breasts. She took off her dark glasses and looked at him, her eyes very blue in the strong light.

'Perhaps it's not as bad as it sounds.'

'Dave's susceptible. Ever since he was ten there's been a girl in his life – usually somebody else's girl. He seems to enjoy complicating his life. There's only a couple of years between us and as soon as I was old enough to date girls Dave got interested and I'd be out on my ear.'

She laughed at his comical grimace, both rueful and indignant, and she guessed that his brother's predatory habits still rankled. Franz had not learned to mask his feelings.

They were always visible – in the intense dark eyes, in the mobile mouth and sudden boyish toothy grin, in the whitening of the wings of his flaring nostrils when he was upset and in the slanting vertical furrow that deepened between his narrow brows in moments of perplexity. His light sun-bleached hair sprang from a broad forehead or fell across it untidily and the loose-limbed way he moved reminded her of a young animal – a yearling with the promise of strength and speed. She thought suddenly: He can always make me sorry or glad just by the way he looks.

'But a widow. That's fair enough,' she said.

'Ah, but he didn't wait till she was a widow.'

Her dark arched brows flickered upwards.

'So he's married against his parents' will. That must be sad. I'd hate to do that.'

'You're an only child. That would make it worse.'

'Could you marry someone – if they were all against you?'

'I might, but I'd be sorry. You see, we're what's called a united family. Perhaps because we were brought up on a rather lonely farm in the Transvaal. We depended on one another. Of course we had to go to boarding school but in the hols it was fun and we could always bring a friend back if we wanted to. Kevin and Mag always used to, but Dave and I had each other for companionship. We quarrelled a lot of the time but we were very close in spite of it. He was always starting things and then getting bored with them while I wanted to carry on and finish the job or game or whatever it was. I'm more tenacious but he's the one with the initiative. He was always thinking up things – like joining a flying club when we were at university in

Johannesburg. We both got our pilot's licence during that time.'

'That'll be useful in Australia. Tell me more about the rest of your family. What's your sister like?'

'Mag? She's a bit taller than you with my sort of face. The Old Man stamped us all. Magda's quick tempered and she talks faster than she thinks but she's awfully warm and kind hearted really. She and Dave are great friends. She's two years older than he is and Kevin's two years older than Mag. Mum was a biennial producer. Kevin was always conscious of being the eldest and rather lofty – still is. He started to earn his living when he left school because Dad hadn't struck it lucky then. Dave and I went to Wits University. But Kev has a natural genius, for making money, for knowing the value of land and property. He doesn't play the share market much. Dave's the one who does that.'

'Successfully?'

Franz chuckled. 'Not very. He was always a mad keen speculator. Money slips through his fingers but he thinks and acts rich, whether he has it or not.'

'And Kevin?'

'Kev's careful. He respects money. He understands it. So does his wife. Colleen. She's extravagant and generous but only within the limits he sets her.'

'Is she nice?'

'Oh, yes. She's right for Kev. He's a strong silent man and she's a breezy chatterbox. Mag brought her to the farm one school holidays when they were both about sixteen and Kev took one look at Colleen and knew she was for him. They have a boy of four now· and another baby on the way.'

'And Magda?'

'No kids yet, unfortunately. She's married to a doctor – a nice chap and good company but he can't help seeing everybody he meets with a professional eye. Once when I had a gorgeous girl – before Dave swiped her – Jules said, 'Pity she's likely to go deaf.' So I asked why and he said, 'Those wonderful blue-white whites of her eyes.' I was mad about her eyes and then I began to wonder if there really was any connection between that eggshell blue-white and the possibility of going deaf.'

'I must have a look at mine,' said Phil. But Franz laughed.

'Yours are all right. They're just plain clear and lovely. Irises blue as the sea – and what a sea!'

'Should we get ourselves a couple of boards and go in?'

'Let's.'

He sprang up lightly and went to fetch the surf-boards from the Hawaiian beach-boy who had just brought in a party of American tourists in the long outrigger canoe. His colleague was teaching a girl in a bikini to surf, but she was so worried about her costume, which tended to slip off in the breakers, that her progress was poor. Beyond the coral reef trimarans and catamarans sailed to and from Pearl Harbor, the beautiful burial ground of American warships.

Together Franz and Phil plunged into the translucent water that was neither too warm nor too cold and he watched with delight as she rode a swell, rising gracefully from her knee to stand on her board and swoop down the crest in a flurry of flying foam. She was good and so was he, for they both came from continents washed by oceans that broke upon long white beaches in lines of thunderous surf.

'Ah, that was wonderful!'

Philippa dried herself reluctantly. 'I suppose we must go in and change. The parents are expecting us on the terrace for lunch. They've gone exploring this morning but they'll be famished by now. I know I am.'

'Me too.'

Franz returned the boards to the beach-boy, a stocky handsome fellow with a dark skin burned almost bronze. He flashed white teeth at the foreigners and said, 'Enjoy yourselves!' They were to hear the words continually in the next four days – from the pretty Polynesian waitresses in their flowered *muumuus* and Japanese sandals, from shop assistants and barmen, from the maids who did their rooms, from the commissionaire of their rose-pink hotel and the girl who sold Franz a *lei* of flowers and shells on their last evening in Hawaii.

'There,' she said, slipping the light garland over Phil's head. 'You look wonderful! Have fun!'

But when she tried to sell Franz one for himself he refused. 'I'm not a man for a halter.'

Mr and Mrs Collins sat on the broad tree-sheltered terrace. Night had fallen and many garden paths were lit by hooded flares on tall crossed iron stanchions, the open flames dancing in the evening breeze, clusters of fairy lights hung in the huge baobabs and magnolias, the Pacific slapped and muttered gently, and, as always, hidden hands plucked at guitars and voices crooned island love songs.

Mrs Collins, a fair matronly woman, dreamy and vivacious by turns, twirled her *maitai* in its long glass with a miniature orchid on the sugared brim, She sniffed the fragrance of rum and fruit with delicate nostrils.

'It's a work of art. Seems a crime to consume it.'

Her broad stocky husband laughed, his thick grizzled hair cropped close above a weather-beaten face.

'Everything here is a work of art and it's intended for tourist consumption. Go right ahead.'

She set the tiny orchid on one side and sipped the *maitai* thoughtfully.

'What's on your mind?' Mr Collins asked.

'I'm thinking about Phil and Franz. You weren't very well advised to get him taken on as a jackaroo at Black Swan. It's only seventy miles from Broken Hill —'

'Seventy miles is quite a way. And when Phil's teaching at the School of the Air she hasn't time to go staying with the Wales at Black Swan. Anyway I had very little option. She'd written to Dominic Wale herself and all she wanted from me was a postscript to say the young man was reliable as far as I could judge. If I'd refused she'd have gone ahead just the same. And resented my attitude and been that much keener on young Morley. He's a pleasant enough young fellow anyway.'

'Too pleasant. We don't want our only daughter marrying a South African and living half a world away from us.'

Mr Collins snorted. 'You women! Marriage isn't on the cards. He's only twenty-two and Phil is twenty —'

'Old enough. The present generation marries young and propinquity is a dangerous thing.'

'Propinquity at seventy miles!'

'They have a Cessna at Black Swan.'

'Not for the use of a jackaroo who wants to date a girl.'

'Franz has a licence to fly. He belonged to a flying club when he was at Los Angeles.'

'You like him, Rose —'

'I do. That's the trouble. I can quite understand Phil liking him so much.'

'Phil's had boyfriends since she was fourteen. They come and they go. Relax, sugar. Here they are.'

He made a sign to the two figures approaching across the lawn between the wavering flares. Franz's tropical Palm Beach jacket was a shade darker than Phil's short white dress of some lurex material that shone with an irridescent glow. Even in her high-heeled sandals she seemed a slight figure beside this broad-shouldered tall young man.

'What's yours?' Mr Collins asked his daughter.

'A Princess Kaiulani punch, Pop.'

'And you, Franz?'

'Whatever you're having, sir. It looks good.'

'That's Planter's Punch. Rum, I can't pronounce all the names of these other jobs. To tell you the truth there are too many frills in this paradise for my taste.'

Mrs Collins smiled. 'As you were saying, Jim, they have a lucrative philosophy. Please the tourist. Foreigners can do no wrong. We could learn something from that in Australia.'

Her husband grunted. Tourism didn't come into his plans for his country.

'Tourism isn't our premier industry and most foreigners come to Australia to live, not to visit.'

His expression had changed, the light eyes in the brown face were suddenly those of a visionary. Phil knew that her father was seeing great stretches of arid emptiness peopled by new Australians flocking to the mining towns his enterprise had created for them. Jim Collins had spent his

life as a bushman and a prospector and his mineral discoveries, his vision and enterprise, had opened up vast areas
of North-Western Australia to new immigration and the
exploitation of natural resources undreamed of ten years
ago.

'Are we dining in the Monarch Room?' asked Mrs
Collins. 'There's the hula hula and that fabulous diseuse who
sings the Hawaiian ballads so beautifully.'

'Sure, if you like,' said her husband amiably. 'This is
your holiday. You choose.' His business in America had
gone well. American capital was one of Australia's life-
lines and Jim Collins had recruited plenty for his mining
schemes.

'Nothing more?' asked the little waitress in the gaily
patterned *muumuu* when they rose to go. 'No, well then,
enjoy yourselves. Have fun and come back.'

They crossed the lawn to the Monarch Room. The cabaret
was highly sophisticated and the *hula hula* dancing was a
glamorous aphrodisiac intended for the jaded palate of the
wealthy visitor. Every muscle of the star dancer was under
separate and perfect control, a solo performance of its own
until her nerves passed the message of full orchestration to
her body at which moment both girl and music went mad
in one wild frenetic belly-dance. The *diseuse* in her turn
crooned the ballads and laments of the islands with spell-
binding emotion. The whole performance was superbly
mounted with the chorus who had surely been Hollywood
trained.

'Strange how sad they are – these songs of the islands,'
said Mrs Collins. Mr Collins said simply:

'They're songs of love, my dear. Too much mooning for

my liking. I fancy something with a bit more pep in it. Now
that dancing! Those girls must really work hard to keep that
fit. If you could get your tummy muscles into that sort of
shape, Rosie, you wouldn't be taking size sixteens instead of
twelves. A bit more exercise and a bit less bridge – that's the
recipe.'

'Look who's talking!' His wife threw a withering glance
at his own stocky frame. Phil laughed.

'You're both fine just as you are. And believe me, Pop,
Hawaiian matrons are balloon jibs in a full breeze – the lot
of them. Franz and I are going to take some exercise now.
We're going dancing in the International Village.'

'Well, then you can say goodnight to us here,' said Mrs
Collins. 'I know my old man. There'll be no going dancing
for me. He's Mr Cinderella.'

In the small hours of the morning Philippa sighed. 'The
band's packed in and I guess we should be getting back. We
leave early tomorrow.'

'Let's walk back along the beach,' Franz said. 'I'll carry
your sandals and you can walk barefoot.'

'And paddle?'

'Sure.'

They sat on the pale beach in the shadow of a great baobab
tree and she took off her sandals and wiggled her bare toes,
burrowing them into the silky sand. Somewhere a clock
chimed three notes of music. A guitar still thrummed, and,
as the night advanced, the songs grew sadder. The wash of
the sea was soft, for the rollers here did not burst on the
beach but dissolved into the shallows leaving quiet water
between the surf and the shore.

'Tomorrow we say goodbye,' he said. 'I leave you in

Sydney to go on to Broken Hill and Black Swan – the new beginning.'

'It won't be long before I see you again. I'll be in Broken Hill in less than a fortnight's time to take up my job again.'

'I can't picture you as a schoolteacher.'

'School of the Air is not like any other school.'

'Tell me.'

'I can't. You'll learn about it for yourself when you've been in the outback for a bit. We teach invisible pupils in an empty classroom.'

'Sounds quite spooky.'

'It's the way it goes in the world of voices – the world of great empty spaces and isolation.'

She was lying on her side, her cheek cupped in her palm and he was glad that she did not rise and suggest walking back just yet.

'The people who live there – far from anywhere – they must be tough.'

'They are. Tough and silent – except for the women when they get a chance of talking. It's rare enough and once they get going they find it quite hard to stop. The men aren't like that, even in the towns they don't use two words where one will do.'

'Your father's a bit like that,' he grinned.

She laughed. 'Yes, he's a bushman. He was born and raised on a cattle station – a million acres in the plains bounded by the Hamersleys. He went to school in Perth and university in Sydney and he knows a lot about minerals. When he went back to the station he became a prospector. I guess he's explored every inch of those mountains on foot, on camel-back, by jeep, by air. And now it's paid off. That land is a vast Aladdin's Cave – and they used to call it the vacuum of the North-West.'

'Your old man certainly worked for his success. Mine was luckier. Gold was found on Blue Horizon by a company with an option on it, my father had the mineral rights and he just sat back and cashed in on royalties. But I guess they're both tough as old boots. Dad made a good thing of farming grain and cattle and he really loved the land. Those were his productive years – the years at the first Blue Horizon.'

'And now – is he happy to be retired?'

'He hasn't enough to do.' Franz laughed. 'So he spends his time interfering in the lives of his children. He'd like to control all our decisions – our destinies —'

'Like a Victorian father.'

'Yes, and it doesn't work out these days.'

'If he pays for your education he probably reckons he has a right to help you decide how to get the best out of it.'

'That's how he sees it. But we don't. There'll be a big showdown with Dave marrying this widow in a hole and corner sort of fashion. No proper church wedding, no parental blessing. I'd like to be there now.'

'I'm glad you're not.'

'Truly?'

'Truly.'

He flung an arm across her and drew her to him. The scent of crushed frangipani was sweet and strong in their nostrils as the *lei* of flowers and shells was pressed suddenly against her breast. She moved to pull it over her head and he took it and tossed it towards the sandals where they lay together on the starlit sand, a palely glimmering still life, shadowed by the drifting dapple of the baobab leaves.

'There are supposed to be ghosts in these baobabs,' she whispered.

'Friendly ghosts,' he said as he covered her lips with his.

3

BLACK SWAN

THEY FLEW OVER THE VAST PACIFIC OCEAN, CROSSING the invisible date-line whereby a day slipped out of the calendar by some magical trick of mathematics, and that same night they were in Sydney, a densely winking embroidery of lights spreading inland from the rainbow arc of Sydney Bridge to the foothills of the Blue Mountains.

The Collins family were met by cousins who put them up for the night at their home in Rose Bay and included Franz in their hospitality.

'The children are away with friends for the holidays – up in the Snowy Mountains – so we've plenty of room,' said Mrs Castle, a well turned-out woman who seemed younger than her forty years. Her husband was brusque and quick and Franz was surprised to see how much he did to help his wife about the home.

'Why don't you stay on with us for a few days?' Mr Castle suggested to Franz over a real Australian breakfast of eggs and bacon and chops next morning. 'You can get some of the best surfing in the world round here.'

Franz was sorely tempted to accept the offer but the Wales were expecting him at Black Swan and his plane to Broken Hill left at 11 a.m. Mr and Mrs Collins and Phil were due to set off on their three-thousand-mile flight south to Perth that afternoon. So he thanked his host and declined the invitation.

'Ah, well, another time,' said Mrs Castle, as she and Phil cleared the table. 'You could take Franz to the airport in my car this morning, Phil, if you've nothing else in view.'

'Surely I could get a bus from the city terminal,' suggested Franz.

Phil passed the last dishes through the serving hatch into the kitchen. 'You could, but you won't. I'll take you and show you some of Sydney on the way. It's rather gorgeous with sheer cliffs and beaches, a spectacular harbour and a messy higgledy-piggledy city with old and new, ugly and beautiful, crammed together.'

By the time they reached the airport the thermometer had touched the century and the humidity of late summer dewed their skin.

'It'll be even hotter at Black Swan,' smiled Phil, 'but drier. This continent has fierce summers. There's your plane being called now. You must go.'

He wanted to kiss her but she laughed and shook her head.

'I'm too hot and sticky. Be seeing you in about ten days' time.'

He walked out into the dazzling heat of the apron and when he looked back from the foot of the gangway he saw her dark head still among those at the barrier.

Within minutes he was airborne above the straggling, densely populated city, then the Pacific coast receded and the plane was heading inland over the thickly forested Blue Mountains towards the vast empty plateau of the interior.

Franz had been raised in a continent of immeasurable

distances and varied climates but when he looked down at
the limitless expanse of hot dusty bush he experienced a
sense of immense desolation. The red earth and grey-green
bush was pitted at intervals by waterholes, and here and
there the blades of a windmill flashed in the blinding
light but these only intensified the endless monotony. It
was early afternoon when the bright thread of the Darling
River and the wide blue waters of the Menindee Lakes
reflected the sky and a few minutes and seventy miles
later they came down at Broken Hill, the city of silver and
zinc.

Franz gazed down at the rich curiously shaped hill with
woods and gardens to keep the drifting desert sand from
encroaching on the lonely little city. He thought of Phil
working here in the heart of nowhere, teaching pupils
hundreds of miles from their schoolroom, and it seemed to
him that he had entered a stark harsh world which made
remorseless demands on the human temperament. He found
that he was nervous, afraid of failing Phil and Mr Collins
who had recommended him to Dominic Wale.

The air hostess opened the door to let in a blast of heat,
and, as he followed the other passengers to the barrier gate,
he noticed a slight young man with reddish brown hair and
a lean hatchet face evidently waiting to meet the plane, for
he was scanning the approaching passengers with a slight
frown. His khaki bush-jacket was covered with little flies,
the summer plague of the outback. He seemed oblivious of
them. He wore neither a hat nor dark glasses in spite of the
glare. Suddenly, as Franz appeared at the gate with his suitcase marked F.M., the young man in the bush-jacket
pounced.

'You must be Franz Morley.'

'Yes, on my way to Black Swan station. Would you be Tim Wale?'

'I would not. I'm Doctor Ian Gray, the junior Flying Doctor. If you'll follow me I'll give you the rest of the story later. That's our crate just warming through on the runway over there.' He pointed to a green and white three engined Drover with the words Royal Flying Doctor Service NSW painted along the fuselage and a red cross under each wing.

'Dominic Wale has just all but sliced off two fingers with a circular saw. They're hanging by threads and it's my job to do something about them and bring him back here to hospital where we can operate. The emergency call came through on the network ten minutes ago and Mrs Wale asked me to pick you off the Sydney plane and bring you along. This all your clobber? Fine. Away we go.'

Ian Gray made a gesture of introducing Franz to the pilot, Joe Gibson, who looked down from the cockpit, grinned and tipped an ancient squashy felt hat in greeting. As they flew between the bush and the cloudless sky Ian Gray explained the situation.

'You don't know Black Swan yet, do you? It's about seventy miles north-east of us on a tributary of the Darling. It's a family partnership, not very big by Australian standards. About eighty thousand acres carrying some eight thousand sheep. Have you met any of the Wale family?'

'None. They are friends of Mr and Mrs Collins of Perth. That's how I got the introduction. You probably know Philippa Collins.'

There was a slight pause. 'Phil? Yes, I know her well.'

Franz felt his hackles rise. But Ian Gray went on smoothly. 'Jim Collins is a big wheel in Western Australia. He owns a couple of million acres in the iron-bearing Hammersleys – what they used to call the vacuum of the north-west. That's a long way from here. Phil's an only child and I think she likes working far from home. Independence is important to a girl of her age and temperament. She makes the grade here in her own right and not as the daughter of a mining magnate. But to get back to the Wales. There's Dominic and Mrs Wale and their son Tim, who's a partner. Tim and his wife, Kathy, and their baby, Jane, live in their own set-up across the garden. Then there's Angus Macintosh – Mac – the station hand, who has a small bungalow which he shares with the jackaroo.'

'That'll be me.'

'Sure. And that constitutes your entire community. Everything is mechanized and there's no other labour needed. Coming from South Africa, you may expect to find aborigines, but they'd be redundant on Black Swan. Now, tell me about you. What brings you here and what do you know about sheep?'

'I know very little about sheep. I'll have to learn. We farmed grain and cattle in the Transvaal where I was brought up. I've been studying agriculture in California. That's where I met Phil and her parents. They reckoned I should extend my education to Australia before going home.'

Ian Gray nodded. 'The outback's an experience. That's why I'm doing a stint as a Flying Doctor before settling down to conventional practice. Now you can see Black Swan. Over to our right.'

It was an oasis. The single-storeyed, tin-roofed homestead, the separate bungalows and outhouses, the huge shearing shed, tall gums, water-holes and windmills, and a shallow lake fringed with thick scrub and willows.

'The lake's almost empty now after the summer,' said Ian. 'But there's still enough water for the birds.'

As they lost height the tiny nucleus of life in the surrounding emptiness clarified and broadened. Flocks of sheep were visible in paddocks miles from the house, and, as they landed, a few emus ran across the runway with surprising speed. The lake was covered with waterfowl undisturbed by the roar of the Drover. It was just another bird to them, big, noisy, familiar and harmless. Among the waterfowl rose the long snakelike necks and heads of hundreds of black swans. A couple of inquisitive kangaroos sat up to watch the plane before bounding away through the scrub.

Tim Wale, a tall lantern-jawed young man, was standing beside a station-wagon as they came in to land. He greeted them with relief and they bundled Franz's bags and a few medical supplies into the car and drove off swiftly towards the house.

'How's the bleeding?' asked Ian Gray.

'Under control. Ma's made a wonderful job of patching up his hand.'

'Everything's ready for him at the other end. Doctor Groves will operate as soon as we get to the hospital.'

The main house was long and rambling and the lawn outside it was 'mowed' by Mrs Wale's pet lamb, and was surrounded by flowering shrubs including frangipani, jasmine, hibiscus and camellias. Mrs Wale came out to meet them.

'Welcome to Black Swan, Franz. Glad to see you, Ian. Come this way.'

She was small and wiry with greying dark hair and lively blue eyes.

'Tim and I did everything just as you said, Ian, and Dom seems fairly comfortable. The Codis seems to be looking after the pain for now.'

Dominic Wale was tall and rangy like his son with a lined face in which the crow's feet were deeply etched round the eyes from years of looking into strong sunlight. His receding hair was grey on the temples, but though his face was drawn and his left arm in a sling with the hand heavily bandaged he gave an impression of vigour and authority.

'Good to see you, Ian,' he said to the doctor and then he turned to Franz with a wry smile. 'You've come at the right moment, young Morley, just when I need another hand in more senses than one. Tim and Mac will give you an idea of what goes on – mustering and drafting, inspection of bore-holes and so on. Anyway, I don't expect to be gone long.'

Ian Gray looked at Mrs Wale with his quick smile.

'I gather there's no need for me to undo that bandage now.'

'I think not. I was a nurse, you know.'

'I remember. Will you come in to Broken Hill with your husband?'

'Kathy can come over here and cook for the boys if you want to go, Ma?' put in Tim.

Mrs Wale shook her head. 'No, there's nothing I can do for Dom in Broken Hill. I can get the doctor's report over the network. When Dom's right one of us'll fetch him in the Cessna.'

'Good. Then we'll be off.'

They're tough stoical types, thought Franz, as Tim drove his father and the doctor to the waiting Drover. In a way Dominic Wale and Tim reminded him of his own family. They too were descendants of British pioneering stock tenacious and taciturn by nature with the younger generation more spontaneous and sociable, the product of university life and inheritors of a place in the sun created for them by their forebears.

'Now, you'll be wanting a cup of tea, Franz.' Mrs Wale bustled into the kitchen to put the kettle on. 'Tim'll be back to join us in a few minutes.'

As she spoke they heard the roar of the Drover's engines and Mrs Wale opened the fly-proof door of the back verandah and Franz followed her into the yard. She shaded her eyes with a work-roughened hand as the Drover passed overhead, the red crosses visible under the wings. A cat stretched and yawned and came to rub itself against Mrs Wale's legs and the lamb scampered in from the garden with joyous baas.

'The cat is one of Mac's,' she said. 'Mac loves cats. He's the station hand, cantankerous when he's been on a bender, otherwise all right.'

She rose and cast a last look at the plane, already only a speck in the blue sky.

'I'd have gone with my husband – Kathy could have managed here – she's Tim's wife and capable enough, but Dom hates any sort of fuss.'

'Was it a very bad injury?'

'A clean cut with the circular saw. But luckily the fingers weren't severed completely. I guess Doctor Groves can fix Dom up. He's a good surgeon. We're lucky.'

'It's remarkable – this Flying Doctor Service.'

She smiled but her eyes were suddenly moist.

'We call it our umbrella of safety. When you're in trouble you're never alone. You have the Flying Doctor. And there's the School of the Air for the outback kids. It's all on the same network. We'd be isolated without them. Come along in, the kettle's boiling.'

Tim joined them, and after tea he took Franz to the bungalow across the yard.

'You'll be living here with Mac, but you'll be eating over at the big house. Kathy and I have a cottage across the garden and you'll always be welcome at our place. I mean that. We enjoy a bit of company of our own age.'

Franz's room in Mac's quarter was bare but adequate. There was a homely living-room and a tiny kitchenette and a large fridge well stocked with cans of beer and cool drinks and a few tins of food.

Mac had pale watery blue eyes in a freckled sun-reddened face and a crop of thick sandy hair. He was short but immensely powerful. He'd been six months at Black Swan and no one seemed to know anything much about him except what they saw for themselves. He was a hard worker and good humoured though from time to time he turned surly. Then one day he'd disappear. After a while he'd return, quiet and subdued, and no one would ask any questions. The bush people were by disposition and circumstances uncommunicative.

On the morning after Franz's arrival he and Mac went

over to the big house for their substantial breakfast of cereal followed by eggs and steak, toast, marmalade and coffee. Their smokos – the packed lunches prepared by Mrs Wale – were beside their plates. There'd be no more cooking for the boys till the evening meal. While they were eating Mrs Wale switched on the transceiver in the corner of the dining-room. A voice cut across the static, taking telegrams and messages.

'That's Arthur Nicholls, the radio officer at Broken Hill base,' she said. 'He's in charge of the transmitter. He's our middle man. It's just on eight o'clock, time for the first doctor session. There'll be news of Dom.'

The call sign for Black Swan came onto the air and Ian Gray's voice filled the room.

'Morning, Mrs Wale, I've good news for you. The operation on Mr Wale's hand went well yesterday and he's bright as a button this morning. Says you're not to worry and he'll be home soon. Doctor Groves agrees. There'll be no permanent disability – thanks to your prompt action. You made a fine job of your first aid. Any message for Mr Wale? Over.'

'Thank you, doctor. Just tell him to get well quick, that's all. Over.'

Franz wondered why the formal 'doctor' when she'd called him Ian the day before. But he quickly realized that the network was open and that everything said over it could be heard by every subscriber who happened to have tuned in to the session.

'The network is our grapevine,' smiled Mrs Wale. 'It's how we keep in touch with what's happening all over the outback. We get to know the people at the other stations, and if somebody's sick or in trouble we all know about it.'

Mac grinned. 'That can be embarrassing when symptoms are being discussed but it's interesting – oh, very interesting.'

'Get along with you,' said Mrs Wale. 'And be quiet now. I want to hear how Mrs Donkins' baby is doing.'

She got up to refill Franz's coffee cup at the stove, and, as she put it down, she said with a smile, 'When we join the Royal Flying Doctor network and receive a call sign for the station we promise to regard everything heard over the network as confidential. We use it as a sort of telephone too. There's an hour when the women can call each other up for a chat. It's called the galah session.'

'Wait till you hear a flock of galahs squawking in a tree and you'll know why,' said Mac.

Tim came in, kissed his mother a perfunctory good-morning and suggested it was time they made a move.

'You can come with me in the Land Rover,' he said to Franz. 'We're mustering today. This is my assistant. His name is Marco.' He patted the lively kelpie at his feet and the pretty little sheepdog responded eagerly. 'Marco loves his work.'

As they left the house the heat hit them between the eyes. It blanketed the scrub, the grey-green mulga trees waded in mirage and a haze danced above the red earth. The little sticky bush flies swarmed round them as they got into the Land Rover. Mac and his kelpie had taken the Jeep on a different course. The paddocks were acres wide and far afield and the land was dotted with windmills several miles apart where the sheep had collected in the sparse shade of a clump of willows, a nelia or a eucalyptus. Brilliant parrots and smaller birds rested in the branches.

'No shepherds?' asked Franz.

'Only the dogs,' said Tim. 'We drive and guide the mobs with the Land Rover or the Jeep. They're so gregarious you can't go wrong. Get one mob moving in the right direction and more come from other paddocks and join up. You'll see.'

So, in the great heat of the worst month of the year, Franz began his new job. At the end of that first day he was burnt and bone-weary.

'We're coming over to eat with Ma tonight,' said Tim as he left Franz at the bungalow. 'So you'll meet Kathy and little Jane then.'

By the time he had showered and changed and crossed the yard where the cats and Mrs Wale's pet lamb waited for their supper the baking heat of the day had subsided. He pushed open the fly-wired door of the back verandah and went into the dining-room by way of the airy kitchen. This inner room was comparatively cool and he saw a young woman leaning over a carrycot on the couch. The baby lying in it cooed drowsily. The young woman straightened up and looked up at him with a pleasant smile. She had large grey eyes and fair hair and she wore a thin flowered cotton dress that was a little too tight across the bosom. Franz guessed she was still feeding her baby.

'So you're Phil's friend, Franz.'

'And you're Kathy.'

'Nice to have you here,' she said. 'A family's all very well, but we need livening up.'

'It must be lonely,' he said.

'At times. But don't waste your pity on us. We have the

Cessna and, except for Ma, we can all fly it. Pa used to fly Tim and his brother, Paul, to school in Broken Hill on Mondays and fetch them home for the weekend on Saturdays. Afterwards they went to Sydney University. Paul's jackarooing on a cattle station in Queensland at the moment. Now that *is* lonely. Hundreds of miles from anywhere.'

She adjusted a light absorbent sheet over the baby and sat on the arm of the couch.

'Jane's nearly off,' she said with satisfaction. 'She's really a very good baby. There's beer in the fridge if you'd care to get some. The mugs are on the shelf above it.'

'Thanks. And for you?'

'Sure.'

He returned from the kitchen with two foaming pewter mugs. She took hers from him with a provocative glance that met his eyes gaily.

'Here's luck. I hope you'll survive your outback experience.'

'Same to you.'

She laughed. 'Let's hope so. It's fairly new to me too. I was born in Perth. I'm a Western Australian like Phil. Our families were friends. I'm three years older than Phil. That made a difference when we were kids, but now the gap has narrowed.'

'Do you like it here?'

'It's all right. Sometimes I get restless. Do you know Perth?'

'Not yet.'

'It's a good spot. Green and lovely on the banks of the Swan River. And the sea five minutes away. I miss the sea. We have to make do with Menindee Lakes.'

There was wistfulness in her expressive eyes.

The aroma of roast mutton wafted from the kitchen with onion sauce and mint. Mrs Wale called out.

'Kathy, turn up the transceiver. There may be news of Pa in the evening session.'

Kathy went to the transceiver as Tim strolled in, followed by Mac. The set crackled and presently the voice of Doctor Curran, the senior Flying Doctor, told them that all was well with Dominic Wale. There was a reminder too that the School of the Air resumed its term in the following week and that it would welcome Miss Philippa Collins back after her prolonged vacation in America.

'Miss Collins should come back to us with plenty of new information and ideas,' added the School of the Air announcer.

Kathy flashed a glance at Franz, her eyes brimming with mischief. 'I'm sure she'll come back with some new ideas! So now you can hear for yourself how the network is our gossip sheet in the outback. But somehow they've missed out the fact that there's a South African jackaroo at Black Swan introduced by Miss Philippa Collins.'

Dominic Wale was back at Black Swan before the end of the week, his arm in a sling, but Tim or Franz drove him wherever he wanted to go or piloted him in the Cessna.

One morning, when Franz was at the controls, the older man tuned into the network and suddenly above the inevitable static Franz heard the warm vital voice of Philippa Collins telling her little pupils about California. Dom stole a glance at the young man whose colour had heightened.

'Good, isn't she?'

Franz nodded. 'I'd no idea she could put it over like that.'

'I have to go and have my stitches out on Friday,' said Mr Wale. 'You or Tim could fly me in and we'll bring Phil back here for the weekend. One of us will return her to store early Monday morning. Kathy probably. She likes an occasional shopping jaunt and my wife can cope with Jane for a few hours.'

Franz found his heart racing. It seemed a century since he had seen Phil. Mr Wale peered down at the red earth misted over by dust raised by a hot wind from distant deserts.

'Circle round that borehole and land on the strip beside it. There's a sheep down there caught in the wire fence.'

They rescued the sheep, made sure the windmill was working and took off again on their tour of inspection.

It was Tim who took his father to Broken Hill in the Cessna, and, while Mr Wale was at the hospital, he collected stores and called for Phil who boarded with Mrs Conway, the Head of the School of the Air. Mrs Conway was a widow with two married daughters and she enjoyed the help and companionship of her young assistant in the home during term time.

The Cessna came down over Black Swan in the late afternoon. Kathy was at the hangar to meet them, Jane astride her hip. She greeted Phil eagerly, looking forward to a weekend of girls' gossip.

'You'll be staying at the big house,' she said. 'But you're coming to dinner with us this evening – you and Franz.'

'How is Franz doing?' Phil asked.

'From what Tim tells me he's coming good. He doesn't grumble – and has it been hot!'

Tim took Phil's arm. 'Want to come to the shearing shed

with Pa and me? Mac and Franz'll be over there in the yards. Kathy has to put Jane to bed and cook our dinner.'

'I'd love to,' she said.

Tim drove the Jeep over the bush as if it were a bulldozer, leaving a cloud of sun-gilded dust in its wake. As they approached the shed the air was full of maaing and baaing as the two kelpies and the two men mustered the sheep in the drafting yards. Tim parked in the shade of a gum.

'We'll leave you here while we give them a hand,' he said.

When the men had gone Phil got out and stood quietly in the shade of the tall tree. She guessed that Franz was unaware of her presence. Mac was operating the three-way gate dexterously, separating ewes from weaners, with Franz helping, vaulting the low fence from time to time to drive the mobs towards the shed. Cloven hooves thudded and pattered in the thick dust as the sheep ringed around and clattered up the ramp and over the grilles into the big cool shed. Soon they'd settle down and all would be silence.

When the drafting was done and the last sheep rounded up Mr Wale came over to join her.

'Franz can drive you home,' he said. 'I'll go in the Land Rover with Mac and Tim.'

Franz strode after him, his bright hair dusty, his face red with heat and sun, his eyes alight with excitement. Phil felt the colour flood her own cheeks.

'Hi, Franz!'

'Hi, Phil! Wonderful to see you.'

They got into the Jeep and he drove her slowly home in the tracks of the Land Rover at a dust-free distance.

'How are you liking it?' she asked.

'Fine. The Wales are grand folk.'

'They are,' she agreed. 'Oh, stop a moment! 'Roos over there. Let's watch them.'

The evening was very quiet now, the unearthly stillness of the bush heightened only by its own voices – the calls of birds, the whisper of a sunset breeze with the dry taste of parched earth on its breath and the rustle of small scurrying creatures in the undergrowth. The kangaroos – a big fellow, his smaller mate and a little joey – were pounding through the scrub to the rim of beyond, their heavy tails like pothooks just skimming the ground behind them, their tiny hands on their chests. But as the car stopped they stopped too and sat up on their long feet and thick tails, listening and watching. A flight of birds passed overhead on its way to the lake, a flock of rose and grey galahs left the boughs of a dead nelia in a cloud of exquisite beauty and hideous squawking, circled and settled again and were quiet.

'Lovelier even than flamingoes,' said Franz. 'I loved the flamingoes we had on our farm at home. Those 'roos really are something – right out of our time and world!'

'The 'roo shooters have to come at least once a year to keep them down,' said Phil. 'They shoot and skin them on the spot and the meat is used for pet food – except for the tails and they make good soup. But it always makes me sad when I see the relics in the bush – a tiny dark hand like a human child's but thumbless, a long foot with one huge claw, or maybe a skull. They're such gentle harmless creatures, but they're grazers and no grazier dare let them multiply or the sheep would suffer.'

The swift dusk was falling and more and more 'roos appeared for they were night-grazers. Franz drove carefully to avoid them. The sunset left its red glow in the west and in the east the full moon was rising.

'We're dining with Tim and Kathy tonight,' he said, as he drew up outside the big house. 'I'll take your bag in and then I'll go across to the bungalow and clean up and come back for you.'

An hour later, scrubbed and sun-bronzed, he fetched her. They strolled across the garden to Tim and Kathy's cottage. The garden smelt of roses and frangipani. She sniffed the air with delight.

'Frangipani – lovely.'

'The flowers of Hawaii,' he said. 'The flowers of your *lei*.'

'Hawaii – that's another world – a holiday world.' She slipped her arm through his. 'You couldn't find a greater contrast, could you? Nothing in common between Australia and Hawaii.'

'Frangipani,' he said, 'and roses, and you. That's enough for me. There or here. Or anywhere.'

He felt a tremor pass through her body but she only said, 'I belong in Australia.' Her voice was serious. It was almost a warning.

They were seventy miles apart yet they were often together. It seemed fantastic to Franz but Philippa took it for granted.

When it was Franz's turn to fetch stores from Broken Hill he usually met Phil for lunch and they snatched an hour or two together before he returned. Sometimes he collected her on a Friday afternoon and brought her back to Black Swan for the weekend.

The Wales were well organized and kept a little Opel car

in the hangar where private planes could park while their owners were in Broken Hill. So whatever member of the family was in town had his or her transport ready to hand. Broken Hill itself was a gay city. Like all mining communities the people were mostly young with young families. There was always something happening. Races, dances or dramatic productions to lure the outback in to town.

Ian Gray was a member of the Drama Circle, so was Phil, and one evening Franz found himself consumed with jealousy to see her locked in a convincing stage embrace with the Young Flying Doctor.

'That must have taken a good deal of practice,' he remarked caustically at a supper party which Dominic Wale gave for the cast after the show.

'Ah, hardly that,' smiled Phil. 'It was only a matter of doing what comes naturally.'

At sports club dances and the races it seemed to be generally assumed that she would be escorted by Ian if he was not on duty. So the Flying Doctor had been – and possibly still was – her boyfriend.

One morning in early autumn Mrs Conway invited Franz to come to a School of the Air session. It was his day for collecting stores in Broken Hill and he was glad of the opportunity to see Phil at her job. The classroom was fitted out like any other with little desks and benches, all new looking, for they were seldom used. On the wall was a large map of the New South Wales, South Australian and Queensland stations served by the School with the various stations flagged with their call signs. The teacher's chair and desk on the low dais were next to the transceiver. At the back of the classroom was a glass partition behind which Arthur

Nicholls or one of his assistants operated the powerful trans-
mission set. Philippa took a long ruler and pointed to one of
the little flags on the map.

'Now this one here – this is our farthest station, Franz,
nearly six hundred miles from Broken Hill. Our pupils here
are Jimmy Cuthbert aged eight, Kate seven and Doris five.'

He watched her intent face, the strong clear-cut profile,
and suddenly he saw a new Philippa dedicated to the battle
against ignorance and isolation. As she turned and smiled at
him, he said:

'What is the Cuthbert station? Sheep? Cattle?'

'No. It's a point on the Wild Dog Boundary Fence.
There's a fence many hundreds of miles long between New
South Wales and South Australia to keep the dingoes out
and it has to be maintained. Those boundary riders and their
families out there are utterly isolated. Their pets mean a
tremendous lot to the children. Jimmy Cuthbert has a tame
galah that goes with him everywhere, even when he rides
with his father in the Jeep along the fence. Every child in the
network knows Jimmy's galah. It's actually talked to us over
the air!'

Mrs Conway floated into the classroom, poised and
gracious.

'You sit on this chair on the other side of the desk, Franz.
The session's just coming on. I'll introduce you to the
children and you can say a few words —'

'Oh, no, Mrs Conway —'

'Oh, yes, Mr Morley! It gives them a new interest. That's
part of our job – to widen their minds and outlook. They'd
love to hear about South Africa, anything you can tell them.
Now then, off we go, Phil.'

To his dismay, Mrs Conway took Franz's co-operation for granted and made a thumbs-up sign to Arthur Nicholls through the plate glass. The morning session was on and suddenly the empty classroom was filled with voices – some two hundred child voices from stations hundreds of miles apart singing their school song in unison.

'Today we have a new friend in the classroom with us,' said Mrs Conway when they had finished. 'His name is Mr Franz Morley and he comes from South Africa where he was raised in the South African outback. He'll tell you a little about it. Now he'd like to greet you.'

Taken unawares, he had at first wondered how he could possibly interest these children, but suddenly, thinking of the three young Cuthberts away out on the Wild Dog Fence on the fringe of the grim deserts of the west, he found himself talking easily and naturally.

'Our sheep farms too have fences – not against dingoes but against the jackals who burrow under them to get at the sheep, and there are leopards who jump over the stone walls of the folds to tear out the throats of the helpless sheep.' He told them of baboons, of the secretary birds who stalk about in search of snakes, of eagles called *lammervangers* – lamb-catchers – and of the honeybird whose sweet voice could lead to a wild bees' nest. He told of the little bushmen of the Stone Age, like the Australian aborigines, who still lived in the Kalahari Desert and stored their precious water in blown ostrich eggs and brought down their prey with poisoned arrows. He opened up a new world for them, different from – yet similar to – their own. 'To us too water is all important – good rains and rivers, neither dry nor flooded, but life-giving.'

As he handed the microphone back to Mrs Conway to a chorus of distant applause he glanced at Philippa in embarrasment. But he saw that she was proud of him and his heart swelled.

When the session was over and he had thanked Mrs Conway and exchanged a few words with Arthur Nicholls he turned to Phil.

'Shall we go to that little Italian place for lunch?'

'I'm sorry,' she said. 'I'm lunching with Ian Gray. He's meeting me here in about ten minutes' time.'

Suddenly his enjoyment of the morning was destroyed. His evident disappointment made her smile.

'He's got a lot to tell me about.'

She led Franz into the playground and they sat on a bench in the shade of an acacia. 'You see, he's leaving here very soon. He's going into partnership with a doctor in Adelaide. I'll miss him.'

'Do you know Adelaide?' Franz asked.

'I have an aunt who lives there. I know it well.'

'Do you like it?'

'I love it.'

'That's bad news,' he said. 'Goodbye for now, Phil. And thanks for this morning. Next time I listen to you on the network – out in the Jeep or in the Cessna – it'll be different. I've come to know a new Phil now.'

'Do you like her?'

'I love her.'

She laughed. 'See you next weekend at Black Swan.'

'Sure thing.'

The following Friday night, after a family dinner at the

big house, Franz and Phil walked across to the cottage with Tim and Kathy who, together, bore Jane's carrycot with the sleeping baby warmly tucked up inside it. The tang of autumn was in the keen bright air by day and in the quick drop of the temperature by night. Rain had fallen and the lake was replenished and alive with birds.

'Will you come in for a beer?' Kathy asked, but Franz and Philippa refused.

Suddenly, as Tim was about to open the door, he paused.

'Listen! The swans are drumming!'

Strange haunting music drifted up from the lake, a thin melancholy bugling. They stood for a few moments in the all-embracing silence, broken only by this fairy threnody of sound, and then the spell was shattered by a sleepy snuffling whimper from the carrycot.

'That's our signal,' said Kathy. 'Don't forget we expect you both here tomorrow night for dinner, and you'll come over in the morning, won't you, Phil?'

'Sure,' said Phil. 'Be seeing you.'

As they turned away Franz took her hand.

'Let's go down to the lake.'

They followed the strange mysterious mating call to the grassy shore of the starlit lake, careful not to approach near enough to disturb the birds.

'Swan Lake,' she whispered. 'There should be a ballet.'

He slipped his hand under her duffle coat and felt the vibrant response of her body.

'Phil —'

'No,' she cut in, quick and taut. 'Don't say anything. Let's go on as we are. Don't do or say anything to change it – to make it serious.'

'But I —'

'No!'

Her finger covered his lips. He took her hand and held it close to his heart and his mouth covered hers. The night smelt of young grass, of earth and water and resin and the light scent Phil used; it quivered with wings and the strange sweet bugling of the swans. Only words were forbidden, as if she feared the admission of his love.

4

STORM

ROUND BLUE HORIZON THE GOLDEN OAK LEAVES
scattered in autumn storms, and coloured children took
sacks and collected the acorns for pig food. The vineyards
were sear on the hillsides, and in Mrs Morley's garden the
last roses clung, limp and battered, to quiescent bushes.

Dave had rented an attractive house only ten minutes walk
from Blue Horizon and Storm awaited the birth of the child
she hoped would be a son and perhaps a key to the still
impregnable heart of the head of the Morley family. For
Dave's sake Mrs Morley did her best to make his wife
welcome in her home but Hector's attitude remained aloof.
Magda too was unco-operative.

'You love Dave,' Mrs Morley said to her daughter one
afternoon, 'but you certainly don't put yourself out to be
pleasant to his wife.'

'She's evil.' Magda's face was sullen.

'You could overcome evil with good.'

'How?'

'Like this for a start.' Mrs Morley touched the pram cover
she was crocheting. 'Do something to please the person you
resent.'

The fitful sunshine slanted onto the corner of the enclosed
stoep where they sat. Magda looked away and out at the
lawn where the labradors chased a squirrel who skimmed

across the grass and up the rough grey trunk of the big oak into the boughs that were the familiar roads and alleys of his life among the doves. Her face lightened and softened as she saw a child scampering towards the house, followed by a young coloured nurse.

'There's Gaby! What a honey she looks in her jodphurs and sweater.'

'She's come to ride with your father,' said Mrs Morley. 'He's very sweet with her. She's a dear little girl, but temperamental.'

'No wonder. Storm bullies her. She has that child completely cowed.'

Mrs Morley frowned. She knew that it was true. Five-year-old Gabrielle was afraid of her own mother. But with her new grandparents and aunt she was relaxed, confident of their affection and approval. It was curious how they had taken Gaby to their hearts, as if, in doing so, they could compensate for the warmth they found it impossible to bestow upon her mother. Even Hector, to her unbounded delight, was teaching her to ride. She was a slight elfin child with brown curls and her mother's amber eyes and Hector found her an apt and fearless pupil when he mounted her on the placid pony he had bought for her and stabled with his own horses.

'Your father's always been good with children,' said Mrs Morley, watching the tall erect elderly man with the child trotting at his side on the way to the stables. Phoebe, the nurse, would go and find Lettie in the kitchen and take a cup of tea with her.

'So long as the children are good with him,' laughed Magda. But it was a thin artificial laugh for she was suddenly pierced with envy. Why should Storm be so blessed – with Gaby and now with another baby on the way while she, who so greatly desired children, remained barren. And Storm despised her. She flaunted her own condition brazenly, or so it seemed to Magda. Most Sundays the two young couples – Magda and Jules and Dave and Storm with Gaby – had their midday dinner at Blue Horizon. Mr and Mrs Morley liked to be sure of seeing their young people often. That weekly family get-together was proof of Mrs Morley's strength and influence. It was a symbol of the outward acceptance of the intruder. But she knew, as Dave did, that her son was still excluded from his father's will and neither of them shared Storm's belief that the coming infant would melt Hector's heart and persuade him to reinstate Dave in order to benefit his new grandson.

Storm never doubted that her unborn child was a son. When it quickened she had taken Gaby's little hand and pressed it against her belly.

'Feel your baby brother kicking?'

The child had nodded. 'Like a birdie's heart.' She had once held a wounded dove in her hands.

'Like that.'

'When will he come, this baby?'

'Your brother will be born on a winter's night when there's thunder and lightning and the sea is high with enormous waves.'

'Elemental violence,' Dave had remarked. 'You crave it, don't you?'

'For birth and death – and sometimes for loving.'

In July she was proved right. She was true to her name and Garth was, in every sense, the child of storm. He was a fine child and his mother gave him birth with triumphant ease. When he was brought to her, clean and wrapped in a shawl, she put out the cigarette she was smoking and held out her arms. She opened the shawl and examined the miniature features that would one day be Morley, strong and handsome, the sturdy body and length of limb.

'Look at him,' she said to Dave. 'He's a magnificent little male.'

The tiny furled fingers found and tightened on her thumb.

'He has your fine hands,' she added. 'And strong.'

Dave felt his throat constrict. For the first time in his experience of his wife he saw true love in her eyes. Not passion, not sensual ecstasy and satisfaction, but a selfless shining love which was, he realized, for her son alone. That afternoon he took Gaby, wildly excited, to the nursing home where she was allowed to look at her new brother who was held up for her inspection behind a glass screen by a young nurse with a mask over her nose and mouth. The nurse's eyes smiled and the baby nodded sleepily. Gaby longed to touch him. She knew that no dolly could ever feel like a real baby. This was her brother – her own. Suddenly she beat her little fists against the glass barrier and burst into tears.

When he was two months old Garth was wheeled in his pram to the Sunday family dinner at Blue Horizon. Phoebe was in attendance and Gaby was with them, proud and pleased.

Hector Morley looked long and gravely into the pram in its secluded corner of the enclosed stoep and Storm watched him with a curiously animal wariness. The infant was awake, moving his little hands outside his bunny blanket in the weak September sunshine.

'Will he pass muster?' Storm asked.

The Old Man turned to her with his acid grin. 'It's not the first time I've seen him, you know. But he's growing fast and well.'

Mrs Morley put an arm round Gaby and said: 'Gaby has a perfect baby brother.'

The little girl looked up at her and dimpled. Mrs Morley bent and kissed her, turning away from the pram. 'Come with me,' she said. 'I've knitted a jacket for your dolly – just like the one I knitted for Garth. Let's see if it fits her.'

Magda went with her mother and Gaby, the little girl carrying her doll. Jules stayed for a moment by the pram, his professional eye appraising the tiny occupant with approval.

'Gaby and Magda are great friends,' he said, with a glance over his shoulder as the child trotted off with her grandmother and her aunt.

'Yes,' agreed Dave. 'No wonder. Mag's awfully kind to her.'

'Mag loves her and lets her know it,' said Jules. 'And Gaby's very affectionate. She responds.'

Dave looked straight at Storm. 'You could try that some time. Affection might get better results than punishment.'

Storm's eyes flashed fire, but she bit her lip and did not retaliate. Garth had begun to cry lustily. She lifted him out of the pram. It was time for his bottle. He was already weaned. Storm did not have to be told to love her son but there were limits. She was possessive, not maternal. He was a splendid little male who would play her game for her to perfection, but her body was her own once more – every bit of it. She turned to Dave, still angry at his implied reproach.

'Call Phoebe! Garth wants his feed.'

Dave reacted sharply to the arrogance of her tone. 'I suggest you call her yourself and give her your own instructions.' He rang the bell and went into the garden where his mother was examining some new rose bushes. Storm shrugged her shoulders and Jules took the baby from her.

'You can be proud of your son,' he said. Her eyes softened. 'I am.'

Now that Storm had borne Dave's son and was accepted at Blue Horizon she set about establishing a social life. The Morley family was well known and, with the stamp of Hector's apparent approval upon his son's marriage, there was little resistance. Storm played her cards carefully and well and did not antagonize the women. For the present she needed women friends, not lovers. It soon became known that the young Morleys liked entertaining and 'did things well', so the sophisticated society in which they moved was quick to forget past scandals. The Morley baby wasn't the first to beat the gun by a long chalk and his parents were fun. That was good enough. But at home, after a drink or two, the gay intriguing mask was apt to slip and Dave began to learn more and more about his wife's uncontrollable temper. Her venom was often turned upon Magda but it was Dave who received most of the poison. So sharp were her attacks at times that he stared at her as if he feared she might be unhinged, an attitude which infuriated her still further.

'Your sister's behaviour with Gaby makes me sick. She's sugar sweet to that child. She wastes her time on Gaby. So does your father, as if they were trying to make up to her for something.'

'Perhaps they're doing just that. You pour out all your love on Garth. Gaby goes short.'

'Not with you. You spoil her too.'

'Partly for the same reason, partly because she's a sweet child.'

'While I'm cruel and heartless, I suppose.'

'You're capable of cruelty.'

'You don't know me very well, do you? You don't really know what I'm capable of, and that frightens you.' Her voice was mocking but her eyes blazed.

'Perhaps it does. Perhaps it makes me wonder about certain things.'

'You'll never know the answers,' she snarled, 'neither you nor any of your sainted family.'

'I'm going out,' he said.

It had become his habit to escape her unpredictable rages by driving into the woods or heatherlands and then walking till he was exhausted. When he returned he often found her asleep in the big double bed. But on those nights he slept in his dressing-room and his dreams were troubled. It was true that he did not really know her. He had mistaken infatuation for love and the road ahead was shrouded in mist just as the road behind was obscure. He was profoundly disenchanted and prey to haunting suspicions. Yet he still loved her enough to make excuses for her. She'd had a bad start in life, he must never forget that – her father, killed before she was old enough to know him, her mother put away, compelled to leave her children in the care of a reluctant aunt. Gaby and Garth must have a good beginning, but already Gaby had begun to show fear of her beautiful mother who acknowledged no law or morality save her own desire. To satisfy her appetites Storm, like the leopard she resembled, would sacrifice any victim. The night was cold but Dave found his brow and the palms of his hands sweating as he lay alone on the narrow divan bed in his dressing-room.

At the end of September Kevin and Colleen invited Dave and Storm to spend a few days with them in Johannesburg. Kevin had certain business to discuss with his brother.

The spring rains had fallen and the tawny winter landscape had turned brilliant emerald and quivered with tall grasses and wild flowers.

Dave and Storm flew up from the Cape, leaving Gaby and Garth at Blue Horizon in charge of their grandparents. Storm believed that the more Hector saw of his grandson the more he would come to love the child so clearly stamped by the Morley blood. She liked being a guest in her brother-in-law's home. As they sat on the patio enjoying their sundowners with the sounds and scents of the highveld spring all about them, she recalled the stormy night on which her son had been conceived. No wonder her child of the thunder and lightning had fire in his veins. Here, she felt herself to be on triumphal territory. Here she had finally and absolutely conquered Dave with the fertile power of her body and the feminine astuteness of her mind.

Colleen said to Storm, 'I'm going to play with the children while Kev and Dave talk business. D'you want to come up to the nursery, or stay and have another sundowner?'

'I'll stay. Give Huddie and Pam a goodnight kiss from me. I'm revelling in being back in the Transvaal. It's so wonderfully alive after the beautiful moribund Cape.'

Colleen said over her shoulder 'Do whatever you like.

Just make yourself at home. Dinner's at eight o'clock. I'm afraid we haven't organized any wild parties for you, but we might go dancing tomorrow.'

She didn't sound keen and Storm realized that here her reputation was still tainted with the unsavoury rumours surrounding Sidney Barralet's death and her own hasty marriage. Her sense of euphoria deserted her and she listened in silence as Kevin told Dave of his latest project.

'I want to buy a farm.'

Dave grinned. 'To offset your taxes.'

Kevin's dark eyes sparkled with amusement. 'Well, why not? You might care to come into partnership with me. We could even include Franz and make it a family syndicate, if he can afford it. There's a magnificent property – about five thousand morgen – coming into the market between Leslie and Witbank. Grain, of course, and a Friesland dairy herd and any crop you like. We must naturally keep the mineral rights because there's always the possibility of gold up here on the Rand, as we have good reason to know.'

'What do you suggest, Kevin?'

'I want you to survey the land and see what you reckon could be done with it.'

'When do you want me to do this job?'

'Within the next couple of days or so. If we decide to make an offer it has to be soon. That's why I got you up here. To discuss it. If we buy we could put young Franz in as manager on a salary and percentage basis. He's mad keen on farming.'

'But Franz is in Australia.'

'We wouldn't be able to take possession for some time, in any case. We could write and put it to him – again depending on your report.'

'What about the owners? Will they want me surveying their property?'

'That's a condition of sale. They know I'm interested, and they've no objection. Actually, I think they'd welcome you. They know the place is value for money.'

'Right, I'd be interested. And there's another thing, Kev. I think we should get young Franz home whatever happens. Especially for Christmas. You know how Mum and Dad love to have a full muster at Blue Horizon for Christmas – the entire family down to the youngest grandchild. The house is geared to it.'

'Yes, I do. We're planning to come to the Cape for a month from mid-December to mid-January. Mum knows.'

'I'm worried about Mum. She's cheerful and sprightly, just as usual, but she seems to be melting away. You'll be shocked how much weight she's lost.'

'Has she seen Doctor Blane?'

'She says so. And she says there's nothing to bother about. The Old Man backs her up.'

'People usually go one way or the other when they get old,' put in Storm suddenly. 'Fat or skinny. Mum's gone skinny, that's all.'

'I don't believe it is all,' persisted Dave. 'And I want Franz back.'

'I'll write to him as soon as you've reported on the farm,' said Kevin. 'We'll get him home for Christmas with the family.'

The family, thought Storm. Always the family! Even the shadow of trouble draws them together. Mum has said nothing, uttered no complaint, she simply happens to have withered while you watch and straight away they plan to rally round. Colleen and Jules are part of it. I'm not. But the pretence is made. Up to a point I'm allowed to talk the family language, but when any of them look at me they're looking at something alien and not quite safe that's somehow broken into the neat little Morley camp. She rose and went upstairs to change and soon Dave followed her.

'This room,' she said. 'Remember it?' She went to the window and looked out at the darkening veld.

'The lightning,' she said. 'That's one of the things I miss at the Cape – the far-off storms, looking across miles of veld to a horizon that sparks and blazes in the night, a live electric band between earth and sky. It's not *your* storm but you're aware of it, even when it's silent, a force of nature, dramatic, beyond control.'

He was beside her at the window. 'That's what you are – electric, uncontrolled.'

'Garth,' she whispered. 'It was here, this room, with the sky flaming and the rains coming. No wonder he's a vital baby, fire and brimstone.'

'You make too much distinction between Garth and Gaby. It's not fair. You should love your children equally.'

'How can I? One doesn't love to order. Gaby's a nice little girl but she bores me. Garth fights me, young as he is. He gives as good as he gets.'

'Gaby is afraid of you.'

'Tsch – that's just it. Garth isn't, he never will be.'

'Storm darling, there's so little peace in you, so little tenderness. You like cracking the whip. You'd do it with the Old Man if he'd let you —'

She cut in viciously. 'He's old and pig-headed, and he despises me —'

'I don't like that word.'

'Nor do I. It's only your mother who keeps him from showing his contempt openly. As it is, he ignores me. But if he had his way, he'd find some means of coming between us. Your mother is the brake. She's decided to make the best of a bad job – not for my sake but for yours – so she keeps a check on all of them, on your father, Magda and Jules. No, Jules is different, he's not really one of you, he thinks for himself, the rest of you think collectively whether you know it or not. Your mother's is the guiding hand. Even here her influence is felt. Colleen doesn't find it easy to be polite to me but she tries. She and Kev have got the message. I'm to be . . . integrated.'

'Then make it easy for them.'

She ran her fingers over his cheek and felt the hard texture of his skin.

'You know something, it rather amuses me to be the irritant in your family. You're all so sure of yourselves, so smug, but you can't be sure of me. You're afraid of my reputation, afraid that someday, some way I'll create a scandal that'll disintegrate the whole precious unit.'

'You hate my whole family, don't you?'

'I don't know Franz yet. He's like you, they tell me. I might not hate him.'

He put his arms round her as they stood at the window watching the flash of distant lightning. Thunder rumbled ominously.

'Not quite a year ago we stood here like this,' he said. 'That was the real beginning.' He wished he could feel some genuine joy in the thought.

She leaned against him, remembering that night and her

return to her sick husband – his nightmares, his helplessness.

'Yes, Dave, that night was unforgettable. That night I was
on the threshold of the great mysteries of life. Love, birth –
and death.'

Her scent fired his blood, her voice had softened, but her
words chilled him. He drew her closer, longing to seek
oblivion in the ancient ritual of the act of love. But he knew
that the wider love between husband and wife was something Storm had never experienced, whatever she might believe. Her whole capacity for love – it might even be selfless
in the last resort – was lavished on Garth. All else was delusion.

Dave completed his survey three days later and arrived
back at his brother's home soon after six in the evening. He
was exultant yet frustrated.

'It's a splendid investment -- everything you cracked it up
to be,' he said, as he helped himself to a whisky and soda.
'And there's a tennis court, a swimming pool and a pleasant
substantial homestead into the bargain.'

'What's the snag?' asked Colleen, when Dave had given
Kevin an account of the lands and the cattle and the mineral
possibilities. 'In spite of everything, you don't seem quite
satisfied.'

He grinned. 'That's personal. They want a high price –
not unreasonable – but fair. And, honestly, I don't see my
way clear to coming in with Kev on the scheme. I'm sure the
Old Man would want a fifty per cent share. It would be
wonderful for him to go there for a holiday now and again
when he gets homesick for the veld, and I know you can
afford twenty-five per cent, Kev, if Mag and Franz go into
the syndicate with you. But unfortunately I'm out.'

Colleen raised her eyebrows. 'But, Dave, only a month ago, when Dad's gold shares hit the roof, he gave his children ten thousand rands each. That should surely help a bit.'

Storm, who had been sitting silent, sprang to her feet, her face pale and taut.

'What was that you said, Colleen? Ten thousand for Kevin, Magda and Franz —'

'And presumably Dave,' said Colleen.

'*Not* Dave!' Storm's fists were clenched. 'There was no ten thousand for Dave. He's not even had a wedding present from his father. Nothing!'

Colleen flushed. 'I'm sorry I spoke.'

'Let me fix you a martini, Storm,' said Kevin. 'I'm sorry about that too. I'd no idea.'

He moved towards the drinks and began to mix a cocktail.

Storm knew that she dared not speak her mind openly before Kevin and Colleen, but she could not resist turning to Dave and saying in an aside: 'Your father is very vindictive. It seems we are to be the poor relations for the rest of our lives because of me.'

He touched her arm gently. 'He doesn't forgive easily.'

Her eyes narrowed as she took the glass Kevin offered her and drank the martini as if it were water. Dave watched her with resignation. Tonight there would be bitter attacks on his father, vicious accusations, even threats to get even with him. He saw the mood building up in her and, in some curious way, her growing fury mitigated the chagrin and indigation he had felt when Colleen had mentioned the gift that his brothers and sister had received while he remained excluded. He turned to his brother and said quietly.

'If I were in your position, Kev, I'd go right ahead with your plans to acquire that property and I think it's worth-while for you to fly down to the Cape to go into the whole matter thoroughly with Dad. You'll be wanting to write to Franz too when you've mulled it all over with the Old Man and Magda. But count me out.'

So it was that Franz received a letter three weeks later that gave him much food for thought. The highveld farm had been bought by a Morley syndicate and he could, if he wished, take up shares in it later. In the meantime he was offered the managership on a salary and percentage basis with a good house fully furnished. It was a chance in a life-time for someone eager to farm in the Transvaal. It was October now and the present manager would hold the fort till mid-January. Then it would be over to him.

The whole idea excited Franz beyond measure, for now at last he had something concrete to offer Philippa. Yet his glow of happiness was threaded through with apprehension. Ian Gray had left Broken Hill and taken the partnership in Adelaide and since his departure Franz had more or less had the field to himself. Of late Phil's attitude towards him had changed and deepened. She allowed him to believe that she really cared for him, but he knew that she still corresponded with Ian, and, even when it seemed that she most loved Franz, he had doubted himself and wondered about the young Flying Doctor who had been her boyfriend long before he had appeared on the scene.

He sat on the steps of the bungalow in the late afternoon and reread his letter from Kevin. 'We need a prompt decision, as you can understand . . .'

The cats snaked round his ankles in the bright spring air,

and a light dry breeze rustled the flimsy airmail paper in his hands. There was no time to lose. He must see Phil and put his hopes and fears to the test.

He looked up as a light step sounded on the cement yard. Kathy, with the lamb frisking at her heels and the baby straddling her hip, stood looking down at him.

'Why so serious? Not bad news, I hope.'

He scrambled to his feet and folded the letter in his hand, slipping it into his pocket. He threw her his wide grin and his eyes danced under the straight brown eyebrows touched with gold. His eyelashes were too long for a man's, she thought, so thick that they always looked tangled, she liked that shadow of a cleft in his chin and the way his nostrils flared and the strength of his neck and width of his shoulders. She was half afraid of how much she liked him. Tim was moody at times and then she sought Franz's company.

'Not bad news, Kathy. Tim was a good postman today. But my brother's letter has given me quite a bit to think about.'

She glanced up into his eyes and said with a sinking heart and a sudden flash of insight.

'You're thinking of leaving us.'

As he did not answer she turned and began to walk towards the house. He fell into step beside her and took baby Jane from her. The child made no protest, just crowed and grabbed at his ear lobe.

'I don't really know what I'm thinking,' he said.

'And you won't till you've seen Phil.' Her voice was edged.

He only laughed as he pushed the fly-proof swing door open.

'Woman's intuition. Shall I let Baa in?'

She shook her head. 'I'll get his milk ready. The carrycot's in the dining-room if you want to put Jane down. You're very domesticated, Franz. We'll miss you if you go. It's always like that in the outback. You make a friend and your friend goes and the loneliness gets you again. This great empty world of nothing but bush and sheep.'

He followed her into the kitchen and watched her take a tin of powdered milk from the shelf. She put it onto the sink with the bowl beside it. Then she swung round with a quick dancing movement – almost a pirouette – and lifted up her hands to draw his face down to hers. She kissed him very lightly on the lips, and, as she turned away, he saw that her eyes were wet with tears.

5

PHIL

PHILIPPA SAID 'GOODBYE CHILDREN' TO THE EMPTY classroom and crossed between the unoccupied desks to the large cubicle where Arthur Nicholls operated his transmitter.

'The static's bad this morning, Arthur.'

Learning to penetrate the static and distinguish the young voices was an essential part of her job. Sometimes it was like listening to a hurricane. Nicholls, bespectacled, middle-aged and comfortably married with four youngsters of his own smiled at her appreciatively. She looked fresh and pretty with her short dark hair and sparkling violet eyes.

'Dust storms in the desert,' he said. 'By the way. There's a message for you from Franz Morley. He'll meet you after the session so will you wait for him here. What's your news of Ian? We miss him since he left Broken Hill.'

'He likes Adelaide and his partner. I think he's enjoying general practice.'

'A young G.P. ought to be married,' remarked Nicholls, his eyes twinkling behind his glasses. He rose awkwardly. The war had left him with an artificial leg to remind him of jungle warfare in Burma.

It was a little after eleven o'clock when they stepped out just as the Black Swan Opel drew up at the schoolhouse. Franz sprang out of it with his wide toothy grin. There was an air of suppressed excitement about him. He looked very young in his khaki shorts with the bright November sun gleaming on his fair hair.

'Hi, Phil! 'Morning, Mr Nicholls. Phil, I've got a few hours to spare and I want to take you to Menindee. The Cessna's being serviced and I thought we could get a Silver City air taxi over to the lakes.'

Her face broke into a smile. 'I could do that. It's Mrs Conway's session this afternoon.'

'Can we give you a lift to the base, Mr Nicholls?'

'No thanks, Franz. I've got my transport right here. Be seeing you.'

He nodded, and limped over to his old grey station-wagon and Phil tucked herself into the Opel next to Franz.

Less than an hour later they were descending over Menindee's shining blue chain of lakes. Bird-filled trees waded in the shallows and white pelicans bred on shores where a century ago the ill fated explorers, Burke and Wills, had encamped before setting out on their attempt to cross the continent from South to North. In those days Menindee, with its small hotel, a trading store and a police post, had been the last link with civilization.

Jake O'Hara, the air taxi pilot, landed smoothly and opened the door of the single engined plane.

'Where do you want to go? I've got my Combi here in the hangar.'

'The old camp on Lake Pamamaroo. We thought we'd picnic there. And maybe you could pick us up around three-thirty.'

'Suits me. Hop in.'

Menindee snoozed in the mid-day heat – a scattering of

tin roofed bungalows, Maiden's Hotel where the explorers had spent their last night before launching into the cruel deserts of the interior, a few shops and the mission where the Flying Doctor held his fortnightly clinic, attended mostly by the families of Greek or Italian market gardeners, a few local inhabitants and aborigines from the tiny settlement on the leafy outskirts of the little town. The explorers' camp was deserted that day, and Franz and Phil settled themselves in the grassy shade of tall gums and willows. A weir overflowed merrily into a dam where the pelicans fished and smaller birds twittered and warbled. The sky was cloudless and the glade smelled of the cool presence of water. A few insects buzzed lazily.

When they had finished their picnic lunch of pies and fruit and light Australian beer, Franz threw the empty beer cans and paper into the litter bin.

'I keep imagining this camp as it must have been a century ago,' he said. 'The Pathan camel man, Dost Mahomet, and his camels, the horses and the tented wagons and the high hopes of men doomed to die. They believed there was a sort of Caspian Sea in the Centre and all the time the inland sea was an illusion.'

She gave a little sigh. 'And there was only the Dead Heart – the thirstland. What drives men on? Explorers of land, mountains or sea? They go on till eventually they die or are killed in nightmare places far from home.'

'Man is the bravest, cleverest and most inquisitive animal on earth. Some instinct drives him on in search of new knowledge and discovery, stepping over the dead bodies of those who went before him. Our own ancestors did it – mine in South Africa and yours here. They crossed unknown oceans to new lands to make a good life for their descendants, and they succeeded.'

Phil chuckled. 'My first ancestor in Australia didn't exactly choose to make his life in a new land. It just happened to be his fate. He stole a sheep one bitter winter in the Cumberland Fells to help feed and clothe his starving family. He was caught and months later he found himself in a convict ship on the way to Australia. Much later his descendants settled in Perth. By the way, you'll be spending Christmas with us in Perth, won't you?'

He sat up beside her, hugging his knees. She was lying on her side in her shorts and shirt, her long legs bare and relaxed, her toe nails showing through the thongs of her sandals, her cheek resting on her hand. She saw his expression change. His face mirrored his moods and impulses and she knew, as she watched him, that she had stumbled upon something important. The reason for their being here, perhaps? She had thought of it as just an impetuous idea engendered by the soft summer brilliance of the day, but it now occurred to her that he had wanted to be entirely alone with her – away from the Hill, away from Black Swan – in this lovely place where no one would be likely to disturb them. His brows were knitted, his dark eyes sombre.

'That's just it, Phil. That's really why I brought you here where we could be quite alone. To talk it all out with you . . . about Christmas, about other things. About you and me. I've had important letters from home. I have to go back to South Africa before Christmas.'

She caught her breath but she didn't move. Everything was very quiet in the glade except the music of the weir and the bird calls.

'My father and my brother, Kevin, and my sister, Magda, have bought a farm – a sort of family syndicate. It's in the highveld – in the Transvaal. Grain and cattle – a dairy herd. Frieslands. They want to put me in as manager. Later, if I care to, I can take a share in the property. Anyway I'll get a cut of the profits and a decent salary. There's a good house too – a home I could take you to. A tennis court, a swimming pool. It's not far from Johannesburg – about the same as Black Swan from Broken Hill. There are little towns near. We wouldn't be isolated —'

'*We* . . . Franz?'

'Phil, I'm asking you to marry me. As soon as possible. Let me take you home with me. I love you so terribly, so absolutely. I have ever since I first met you.'

She was sitting up now, her back against the smooth trunk of a ghost gum. He moved to put his arms about her, but she took his hands and held them away from her.

'No, darling! Don't touch me. That only confuses everything. This needs talking out sensibly, as you said.' She felt his recoil as she let his hands go but she saw his eyes cloud and his strong sensitive face tightened with sudden dread. Her own heart beat heavily with the knowledge that none of this was going to be easy.

'I love you too,' she said. 'But not enough to go to South Africa with you and start a new life so far from my home and my parents. I'm all they have. I can't leave them for ever. I just can't, Franz.'

The healthy colour drained out of his face. 'I thought you loved me. Ever since Ian left you've let me believe that I was the one.'

'You are the one. But marriage —'

'You don't want to be a farmer's wife?'

'Not in South Africa.'

'It's easier there than here. There's always labour and your neighbours are nearer – within a few miles. There's more arable land. It can be a good life. This offer has fallen into my lap. I could never afford to buy a similar property in Australia or to run it with suitable labour.'

'Must you be a farmer?'

'Yes.'

Now she saw the force of his determination in the set of his jaw.

'If you really love me you'll take me as I am and share my life with me.'

'I love my parents too. I owe them a great deal. They've always been wonderful to me and one day they'll depend on me. Life isn't as easy here in Australia as it is in South Africa. You've pointed that out yourself. The old and the young depend on one another much more here. You must see that. When a woman is ill she can't be sure of being able to get outside help. She has to rely on her children or her friends.'

'Your mother has a great many friends and she can afford help. You have to make your own life wherever it may be. Surely you have the courage – if you have the love.'

'I have my loyalties here. Don't you understand, Franz?'

'Yes, I think I do,' he said bitterly. 'When you weigh your love for me in the balance it isn't enough. It isn't worth the sacrifice.'

'If yours were enough you'd settle in Australia,' she said, crisply. 'You'd be the one to make the sacrifice. My father would find you something.'

'I don't want your father's help. My opportunity is waiting

for me. It's a good one. It could hardly be better of its sort. It's what I've been wanting and hoping for all my life. The way I see it, a man's wife goes with her husband —'

'To the ends of the earth. Oh, yes, I know. It sounds fine but doesn't necessarily work out.'

She was sore at his attitude. He made her feel cheap and cowardly instead of noble.

'You say your parents have been wonderful to you – and I'm sure they have —' he went on. 'Why do you think they'll let you down now? If you told them you loved me, that you wanted to come with me, they surely wouldn't stop you. They could visit us. Your father would be interested in South Africa. And from time to time you could fly home to see them. The air has brought far places near. Think about it, Phil. Please think about it.'

He drew her into his arms and spoke softly, persuasively.

'Don't you see, darling, that for your sake as well as my own I must hack out my future on my own territory. I must be my own master in a country where I know I can make good.'

'So I must give up my family and become incorporated into yours? I must leave my country and my friends and go away among strangers.'

'You're brave enough for that, even if it is asking a lot. Love always demands everything, but it gives too. I could make you happy, sweet. We could build a fine life together. I want to take you home as my wife, but we could compromise. Come and see the farm for yourself, see my country and meet my folk – and then make up your mind.'

His lips were on her hair and his hands caressed her. She sighed and lay back on the warm grass.

'Perhaps. I must think ... away from you ... by myself ...'

'Think of you and me, Phil, of a home together, children,
a real life as a wife and mother, not just as a daughter. You're
everything to me – the beginning and the end, my whole
world.'

But she was afraid of the finality of the decision he was
forcing upon her. It was enough to be young and in love.
She relaxed and responded to his touch and soon they were
making love together in the soft aromatic afternoon with
the leaves murmuring overhead and the white pelicans
fishing under the willows. But this time their loving had a
new quality, a fierce hunger and passion they had not known
before, as if they were both afraid that it might be for the last
time and that nothing would ever be quite the same again.

In the few weeks that followed they spent every moment
they could together. Kathy seemed to understand, and so
did Mrs Wale, and Phil was at Black Swan most weekends.
Franz had told Dominic Wale that he must be home for
Christmas ready to take over the management of the new
Transvaal farm in January.

'It's a wonderful prospect for you, Franz,' Dominic said.
'Tim'll envy you being in complete control of the family
syndicate. No old boss-man to push you around.'

'I'll need advice and then I'll get it from my father. He
was a first class farmer in his day. I can draw on his experience.'

'We're all going to miss you,' said Mrs Wale. 'Phil too.
To go to South Africa you fly via Perth, don't you?'

'Yes,' he said. 'Phil and I plan to fly from here to Perth

together when she begins her Christmas vacation. I'll spend a couple of days there before going on to Cape Town.'

'You should take her with you,' laughed Kathie once when they were alone. 'It's dangerous to leave her. She's very attractive.'

'I wish I could. Maybe she'll come and visit us later – in her June holidays.'

'Lucky Phil! By then you'll be in your own house on your own land.'

'I hope so.'

She sighed. 'I'd love to travel.'

'You and Tim will always be welcome if you come my way. And little Jane.'

'Ah, well, who knows? Maybe one day we will.'

The bush flowered with the scarlet and blue of spring, the shearing team came to Black Swan, thirteen strong, and camped out near the big shed, and at night they sang the old shearers' songs round their camp fire. Then one day they were gone, leaving the shorn sheep, a good wool clip and the silence of the outback broken only by the rustle of the wind, the calls of birds and the magical drumming of the swans. December came with the beginning of the great heat and Franz said goodbye to his Australian friends and boarded the plane to Adelaide with Phil. Adelaide, between the Pacific and its undulating vineyards and orchards, was a pretty city. Franz wondered if Phil pictured it as a possible home – with Ian Gray. When they landed Ian was there to meet them, lively and spruce in spite of the heat and obviously pleased with his growing city practice. Franz was stabbed by a sharp pang of jealousy as Ian and Phil talked about his work and his future and about their mutual friends with the easy intimacy of a pair with everything in common. Being with them made him feel a foreigner and he found an excuse to wander away and leave them alone together while they waited for the Perth connection to be called.

That evening the Jet flew over the arid endless waste of the Nullarbor Plain, leaving South Australia and the Pacific behind and crossing the Darling range of Western Australia to land outside Perth, the city of parks and hills on the banks of the wide Swan River. The lights of Perth and the adjacent sea port, Fremantle, blinked up at the stars and the Indian Ocean washed long white beaches silvered by the moon.

Mr Collins was there to meet them and half an hour later they were unpacking their bags in Phil's home on the river road. The night was languid and sweet scented, cooled by the wide sheet of water. The murmur of traffic was in their ears, the windows of houses glowed close to one another and the vast stillness and isolation of the outback was a thing of the past.

Kathie Wale had kissed Franz lightly on parting. 'You'll never come back,' she'd said.

He knew it was true.

In Perth Franz felt his sense of loss and apprehension deepen. On the morning after their arrival Phil was instantly re-absorbed into a life in which he had no part. Her girl friends came to welcome her and he was conscious of their amused inquisitive glances in his direction. In the afternoon they went to the Yacht Club and he discovered that Phil was an expert sailor.

'Everybody sails here,' she laughed. 'From the age of five.'

In the evening they went to a barbecue and it seemed that he would never get her to himself again. But the next morning – his last – they drove over to the long beach at Cottesloe and they surfed and then ate their picnic lunch under a rough canvas shelter that shaded them from the sun blazing so fiercely on sand and sea.

'When will I see you again?' he asked. 'In the winter holidays? You will come to South Africa then, won't you, to stay with my people at the Cape and with me on my farm up-country. I'll take you to the Kruger Park and show you our wild life – elephants, lions, giraffes, every buck you can think of. There are so many beautiful places I can take you.'

She was tracing patterns in the sand with one finger, her face serious and withdrawn.

'Franz, my darling,' she said sadly. 'It's no good – this make-believe. It won't work out. I'm not coming to South Africa next year. I belong here. You belong there.'

'We belong together.'

'We *have* belonged together – for a little time – a lovely time. But it's over now. Tonight, when you fly to Cape Town, it's the end for us.'

'It can't be. We won't let it be!'

'We must. I've faced it – why can't you? Deep down I've known it since Menindee when you asked me to go to South Africa with you. Perhaps I am a coward, perhaps I love my own people too much. Perhaps I'm just not ready for the responsibility of marriage. I can't analyse my feelings.'

'You can't really know them till you've seen my home and met my people. At least come and see what I'm asking you to share!'

'It's no good,' she said again. 'It would only be a sort of cat and mouse game. We must make a clean break. A person needs great confidence – and a sort of callousness – to give up everything. All this is part of me —'

'Am I not part of you?'

She looked at him with her eyes so soft and warm that his head whirled and his heart lurched and melted.

'You always will be, Franz. Two people can't mean as much to each other as we have without it leaving a permanent mark. You'll be part of me all my life – like a scar. But the deep wound will heal – it must.'

'Can you be sure of that? I can't. The wound of letting you go won't heal for me and leave that nice neat scar you talk about. Those are just words. Love isn't like that.'

'Darling,' she said. 'What do you know about love? You're twenty-two. I'm twenty. We're better free. There's all your life before you – other women, other loves.'

He seized her and held her tightly, tasting the salt on her skin and her tangled hair. The gulls, who had pecked at their crumbs, flew away with a swift rush of wings and she put her arms round his neck and drew his face down to hers.

'Franz, Franz . . . forgive me. But today must be goodbye. It's better that way. It has to be.'

He felt her tears warm on his cheek, but he knew that she meant what she said and that no words of his would shift her.

Hector Morley met his son at D.F. Malan Airport the following night. It was over two years since Franz had left home and he was shocked to see how much his father had aged. The Old Man still carried himself with proud assurance, but his hair and moustache had whitened, his high bridged nose was pinched and the furrows from cheekbone to jaw had deepened.

'Where's Mum?' Franz asked as they waited for his baggage.

'She's waiting for you at home. She tires very easily these days. Kevin and Colleen and the children arrive for their Christmas holidays tomorrow. We'll have a reunion dinner then. All the family.'

'And I'll meet Storm?'

Hector's face hardened. 'Naturally.' He spoke curtly and Franz knew better than to pursue the subject.

'Shall I drive?' Franz asked as they put his suitcase in the boot of the car.

'If you like.'

Franz drove fast and well along the Somerset West road between the mimosa covered Flats. Here and there a vineyard shadowed the slopes of a dark hill and the jagged mountain peaks gashed the starry sky. Ten minutes later they turned into the avenue of gums heavy with clusters of white, pink and scarlet flowers. The jacarandas were a mass of blossom, the roses bloomed in their midsummer glory and the lights of the house welcomed them.

Mrs Morley came out to meet the car, smiling and frail. Franz parked it under the tall date palm and sprang out and hugged her, but with an unfamiliar gentleness, for she seemed to him sadly light and brittle. The bold spirit still shone in her dark eyes but the substance had dwindled to a tiny bundle of slender bones. He was deeply moved and could not trust his voice. Then he became aware of Lettie standing behind her and Elijah beaming broadly and waiting to take his bag.

'It's time Master Franz came home,' said Lettie. 'Two years is too long to be away.'

Franz recovered himself and laughed as he took her thin brown hands.

'It's good to be back, Lettie. Good to see Elijah too.'

He flung his arms about his mother's shoulders as they went into the house and when he saw the contentment shining on her small lined face he understood for the first time, why Phil had baulked at the decision to leave her home and her parents, why she had refused the temptation to come to South Africa, why she had insisted on a clean and absolute break. At the thought of it his heart twisted and the joy of homecoming faded.

'Are you all right?' said his mother. 'You look tired.'

He smiled down at her. 'I'm fine. It's great to be back. Christmas with all the family together – that'll be wonderful.'

'Yes.'

She smiled back and suddenly he knew that she too was hiding something. Did she fear that this would be her last family Christmas? Or was he just weary and over-sensitive, seeking reflections of his own pain in others?

Whenever Jules Strauss was part of a Morley gathering he found himself studying the members of the family with interest, affection and a curious sense of detachment. Close as he was to them, their collective influence could not touch him. The Morley men were farmers or speculators in real estate, or both – the natural product of a young country – whereas he was a doctor, a man more concerned with the anatomy and psychology of his fellows than with the potentialities of cities.

'You look at us from outside,' Magda had said once. 'As if we were specimens.'

'Interesting specimens. Your father, for instance. He's self-opinionated, quite a dictator, always determined to make a success of whatever he undertakes – and he expects his children to do the same. He made his mark as an enterprizing farmer before he struck it lucky and re-tired, so he can fairly pat himself on the back. He's ruthless in many ways and he doesn't mind letting the sun go down upon his wrath. He holds onto a grudge like a bull-dog.'

She picked on the word 'ruthless' and repeated it.

'Ruthless – but affectionate, nice with children. They love him – even Storm's children.'

'That's it. Children are part of the patriarchial pattern. You know, sweetie, people's behaviour is largely condi-tioned by the bodies God gave them. Your father is bigger than his sons in every way. A handsome man of six foot three should be dominant. He must stand straight and think straight because, wherever he goes, he'll be noticed. Your father is a born boss-man.'

She'd been enthralled. She could discuss her own family interminably. 'Mummy would agree with you there.'

Jules' blue eyes had softened. 'Of course. Your mother has all the natural wisdom in the world. She sees your father's faults, doesn't criticize them and very often she mitigates them by her own actions —'

'As she does with Storm.'

'Just so. Your father and Storm are irreconcilable. Your mother is the buffer.'

'I swear Storm's evil. She's capable of anything but Mum believes you can overcome evil with good – whatever that may imply.'

'She tries to do just that, and she may succeed. She's very kind to Storm.'

Jules remembered that conversation now, at the reunion dinner for Franz. Hector and Mrs Morley had led their guests onto the stoep for coffee. The wind had dropped and the summer night was hot and still except for the chirping of crickets. The garden scents of tobacco plants and stocks drifted through the open sliding windows to mingle with the fragrance of freshly ground coffee bubbling in the big glass percolator. Mrs Morley liked to make her coffee herself. She sat behind the big silver tray and poured the strong coffee into the small china cups while Colleen, Magda and Storm passed them round, offering cream and brown sugar. It was all part of a familiar ritual. Dave poured the rich fruity Cape liqueurs.

'Bran der Hum for me,' said Jules, and sipped the tangerine Van der Hum thinned and strengthened with a dash of liqueur brandy. He sat on the couch beside his mother-in-law, acutely aware of the happiness that radiated from her at the return of her youngest son.

'Franz has filled out,' Jules remarked. 'No longer a lad any more. He's really rather a magnificent young animal.'

The smile she gave him was conspiratorial. They shared a secret forbidden to the rest of the family. Having Jules know about the specialist's verdict was a source of immense comfort to her. Even Hector had not been told. She had been adamant about that. 'And you'll keep it from Magda,' she had made Jules promise. He had nodded.

'It's a professional confidence.'

Franz was lighting a cigarette for Storm. She sat on the arm of a chair and he looked down at her bare shoulders as

he held the lighter for her. As she drew on her cigarette and
lifted her head Jules observed the pure line of neck and chin.
She was exercising her attraction on her young brother-in-
law, oblique eyes enticing. Kevin joined Franz and Storm,
anxious to discuss the farm.

'It's called Golden Grass,' said Kevin. 'It's a good name
and we won't change it.' Dave and the Old Man soon
gravitated towards them and Storm drifted away in the
direction of Colleen and Magda.

'There you are,' said Mrs Morley. 'That's what always
happens. The men herd together to talk business or farms
and the women are left to gossip about clothes, babies and
servants.'

'And very lucky they are to possess such things to talk
about.' Jules' eyes rested tenderly on his wife. The strong
Morley features she had inherited did not make for beauty,
but her lively high spirited face had softened of late and she
had begun to veil her instinctive hatred of Storm in an effort
to please her mother. Instead of open conflict there was now
an armed truce between the two young women.

'Dave's getting too thin,' said Mrs Morley. 'He's smoking
too much and he's developing nervous tricks. He picks
things up and puts them down for no reason, he's always on
the prowl. Even if he sits down he's restless, tapping his foot
or drumming his fingertips on the arm of his chair.'

'I've noticed that. It's not surprising, he knows that his
wife creates friction or restraint in his family and he loves
his family. The tension must react on his nervous system.
He's carefree and impetuous by nature and now he's an
extrovert turned inside out by force of circumstances. He
hardly knows what's hit him.'

'I wonder what will happen when . . .'

Jules covered her small hand with his.

'No,' he said. 'We're not thinking on those lines tonight. Magda has some very exciting news to tell you. But it's as much as my life is worth to forestall her.'

'I know, my dear. She found an opportunity to tell me before dinner. It's marvellous. At last!'

'At last,' he said. 'After four years of waiting – and fearing.'

'And for me,' she said, 'it's another thing to live for. I'm so happy for you both.'

'Remember, it's a secret,' he said. 'Only you were to be told.'

She looked up and her glance followed his. Colleen was leaning across the coffee tray, her eyes amused.

'If I help myself to more coffee will I interrupt a big flirtation?'

Jules laughed. 'Yes, bless you.'

'Don't worry,' she said. 'I'm going to break up that pride of lions over there. A handsome lot, aren't they?'

She joined the men, coffee pot in hand. 'Anyone here for more coffee?'

'I'm a buyer.' Franz held out his cup.

'It's fun having you back,' she said as she filled it. 'Dad and Kevin are very keen on the new farm. Magda too. When will you take it on?'

'I'm planning to fly to the Transvaal early in January. There'll be an overlap of about a week with the present manager.'

The party had changed its formation and gravitated towards Mrs Morley. Hector looked at Franz with approval.

'I envy you, my boy,' he said. 'I'd give a good deal to set the clock back and begin all over again with Blue Horizon on the veld. How about you, Marie?'

His wife beamed up at him.

'What woman of my age wouldn't recover her youth if she could? It was a good life.'

'One thing puzzles me,' said Franz. 'Dave surveyed the property and wrote a glowing report but he isn't in on the family syndicate.'

'We can't afford it,' grinned Dave. 'It's as simple as that.'

'And why not?' cut in Storm, her low husky voice suddenly strident. 'Because Dave had no share in the ten thousand rands his father handed out to his other children! There's something you'd better remember, Franz. It doesn't pay for a Morley to marry without the blessing of the head of the house. Never make the mistake your brother did!'

Mrs Morley rose and put her hand on Storm's shoulder. 'That'll do, my dear. We are here to welcome Franz tonight – not to warn him of improbable dangers.'

Hector ignored Storm. She might not have existed as far as he was concerned. He said: 'It's a beautiful night. I'm going to smoke a pipe in the garden.'

Dave reacted sharply to his father's attitude. He slipped his arm through Storm's. 'We should go,' he said. 'Phoebe is baby-sitting tonight till we get back but she has a boy-friend who fancies my whisky and I don't quite trust them on such a lovely evening.'

Magda looked at her husband. 'Jules has an early morning tomorrow. He's assisting at an operation. We should be getting along too.'

So that was what Storm could do, thought Franz. Disintegrate everything.

Storm brushed her mother-in-law's cheek with her painted lips and Mrs Morley returned the light embrace.

'Good-night,' she said. 'Send Gaby over to see me soon.'

'I will,' said Storm, and it occurred to Franz that this was only one of many scenes his mother had averted for Dave's sake. Suddenly he wished with all his heart that his mother could have known Phil. It was a futile thought and painful. The party was at an end, and so was his love affair with Philippa.

'I won't even write,' she had said to him. 'What would be the good?' She had made it all terribly final. His pride had forced him to accept the total break.

The two young couples had left, his mother had gone upstairs and his father and Kevin were strolling on the lawn. He'd joined them and they'd made plans for Golden Grass. If only those plans could have included Phil! He remembered her as she had looked at Perth airport the day she had seen him off, her face pale in the strong light, her eyes sad as she said goodbye. She had clung to him for a moment at the barrier and then she had turned quickly and left him without a backward glance. That had been the worst moment in all his life.

6

RIFTS

FRANZ LOVED GOLDEN GRASS THE MOMENT HE SAW it. The undulating mealie lands, laced with vegetable crops and lucerne, fell away from the house to a far horizon. The dairy herd grazed in the valley near the dam, fringed by mature abundant willows, and the tin-roofed homestead was sheltered by gums, cypresses and a blaze of vermilion kaffirbome – coral-flame trees they were called in Australia. At the side of the house was a swimming pool and tennis court, and a windmill clonked like a giant metronome to the music of the breeze that ran through the grain, constantly changing its colour and texture like wind on the face of quiet water.

Colleen had helped him to furnish and decorate his new home and when it was done she'd said:

'There, it's comfortable and attractive. All it needs now is a wife. As it is, you'll have to count on Solomon to look after you.'

She had found him his houseboy, who had a family in the compound and who sent his children to the Bantu farm-school over the hill. An old Bantu gardener, Pampoen, sang to himself as he watered the little garden at the unhurried pace that was the life rhythm of his people when they were not stirred to sudden passion. His nearest neighbours, Pierre and Zirelda Malan, lived a few miles away at Deep

Donga over the rise. They rented the farm from the Golden Grass syndicate as did various other farmers roundabout. They hired the harvester, too, each year.

To Franz the loneliest, but the loveliest time, was the hour of sundown when the black and white Frieslands went to the dam. As the spectacular sunset flamed in the sky duck and geese were silhouetted above the water, red and yellow finches twittered in the rushes, and sometimes a golden oriole balanced delicately on the top strand of a wire fence, or a pair of green bokmakieries called to one another with bell-like cries. In the cypresses flanking the house doves cooed and the dry resinous scent of grass and gums was carried on the breath of the breeze. It was then that he remembered Black Swan and Philippa, and his longing for her washed over him in aching waves.

Kevin and Colleen often came to Golden Grass for weekends and at Easter Magda and Jules spent a week with Franz. In August, after the birth of Magda's son, his parents came to stay for a fortnight and Franz and his father discovered new worlds in common.

'How do Mag and Storm make out these days?' Franz asked his mother once, when they were alone.

Mrs Morley let her knitting fall into her lap and she looked down from the sunporch at the pale threadbare mealie lands, reaped and harvested and ready for the plough.

'Magda became very fanciful during her pregnancy. She took to avoiding Storm. She even made excuses to dodge our Sunday family lunches towards the end. She said Storm had the evil eye and could harm her unborn child. Have you ever heard such nonsense?'

'Frankly, no. But Mag's always had more imagination than's good for her.'

'Yet she's genuinely fond of Gaby and Garth, especially Gaby. The child goes to school now – a glorified kindergarten – and we're glad of it. It keeps her out of Storm's way in the mornings.'

Mrs Morley spoke calmly but Franz could see the anxiety that she tried to hide. The peace and unity of the clan had been disrupted since the advent of Storm and his mother feared the future. She was frailer than ever physically, but her understanding of her children seemed heightened as the outside world gradually fell away, leaving her more and more deeply entrenched in the core of her family life.

'A curious and rather sinister thing happened to Magda after little Hector was born,' she said. 'You know the usual wave of flowers that descends on a mother with a new-born baby, well, among Magda's beautiful bowls and bouquets was a wreath with little mauve and white everlastings, finished off with a posy of white roses and a satin bow. Think of it, Franz, a wreath!'

'A wreath! It must have been a mistake.'

'It was a very odd mistake. There was no card except the florist's and it was clearly addressed to Mrs J. Strauss. No message or sender's name. It was anonymous like a particularly horrible anonymous letter. Of course Jules rang the florist and they said the lady – they didn't know her – had paid cash and given no name. She was tall with reddish hair, good-looking. She had ordered the wreath to go to Mrs Strauss' address and said that the people were expecting it and there was no message. It's a shop none of us know – somewhere up in Long Street. Magda is convinced it was

Storm. Jules and I managed to stop her making such a dreadful accusation, but she said to me, "I told you Mummy. Storm's the sort of person who might make little figures and stick pins into them. That hateful wreath – it was what she wished for us. Death. Me? My baby? Someone we love? I don't know. But it was a death wish and she did it on purpose to hurt and frighten me."'

'Do you believe that?'

'I don't know. Like you, I prefer to think it was a macabre mistake of some sort. The trouble is I believe Mag is afraid of Storm, yet she's still very sweet to Gaby and the child adores her. Sometimes I take Gaby to Mag's flat myself or they meet at Blue Horizon. Storm makes no objections. In fact I think she's indifferent to Gaby. All her affection is centred on Garth, who is undoubtedly a child of great character and drive, young as he is . . .'

'I don't understand why Storm should play such a nasty and cruel trick on Magda,' said Franz.

'She's vindictive,' said his mother. 'As if she'd heard in some way that Mag reckoned she had the evil eye, I suppose it's just possible —' Mrs Morley broke off and shook herself. 'As you say, the whole thing's absurd. Don't let's dwell on it. Tell me about you. Wasn't there a girl in Australia?'

'There was. But that's over now.' His face had hardened.

'Yet you have a snapshot on your desk. I suppose that's the Phil you used to mention in your letters.'

'Yes.'

'She has a lovely face. Not chocolate box but full of character.'

'Not enough character to leave her home and come out here.'

'It's asking a great deal.'

'You'd have gone anywhere with Dad.'

'I was sure of myself – and him. You're very young. What age is she?'

'Twenty.'

'You've plenty of time – both of you.' Her tone was envious. 'All your lives before you.'

'Our separate lives,' he said. 'Let me get you a sundowner, Mum.'

'I'll wait for your father.'

She saw him with his long attenuated shadow come up through the rough garden. He carried a heavy stick and the wind ruffled his white hair. Franz's spaniel trotted at his side. Mrs Morley smiled.

'He's happy here. It's nostalgic – like recovering a little bit of his youth. Men may say what they like, my dear, but I don't believe they ever resign themselves to retirement. It's the last bridge but one, which is probably the hardest to cross.'

When his parents returned to the Cape the house seemed very empty and Franz often sought the company of his neighbours, the Malans. Pierre and Zirelda Malan were a young Afrikaans couple who always made him welcome at Deep Donga and it was pleasant to go there at the end of a long day in the lands. They had much the same problems and grumbles and the same pleasure in good crops. If locusts attacked Deep Donga they attacked Golden Grass too and the same rains were vital to both properties.

The spring rains had not yet fallen when Franz stood on the steps of his house and looked out across the mealie fields to the clouds banked low on the horizon. Tonight perhaps?

Pampoen was watering the garden parsimoniously when Franz called to him in Afrikaans.

'Pampoen! I want you to saddle Star for me. I'm riding over to Baas Malan for supper and I'll need the horse in half an hour.'

'Ja, Baas.'

Pampoen was, in many ways, as much a pumpkin as his name. He tended the soil and did as he was told and left such business as thinking to others. He had no watch. 'Half an hour' meant for him the little space between the red sky and the grey dusk, time in which to amble peacefully up to the stables and saddle the white stallion for his master and lead the fine animal down to the garden gate. And when the young baas had galloped away he would stroll quietly over to his hut and eat the mealie-meal his little wife had prepared for him with perhaps some meat added to it. His pot-bellied piccanins would share the evening meal and so would his old wife, which was an imposition as she very well knew. But she was fat, lazy, good tempered and did nothing for herself if she could persuade his little wife to do it for her. The old woman had proved to be barren into the bargain, a bad bargain, hardly worth the cattle he had paid her father. He spat contemptuously. But he had loved her once and they had laughed and made love together when she had been a beauty with broad soft lips and bouncing curves. He felt in his pocket where he had some snuff for her. Snuff and beer were her pleasures now. He still liked to talk to her in the shelter of the reed screen on sunny days. She was wise, as an old woman should be. In a way he, Pampoen, was more content than his young baas. He had a wife for company and a wife for pleasure, a mealie patch and some fat cattle. The young baas had his blessings – his herd, his land, his stallion, his dog and a fine house. But no woman sang in that house and no children played in the garden. What was he waiting for? No young man should waste his youth alone. What use were good crops if the best crop of all – sons and daughters – was missing?

Franz, whose sentiments were much the same, cantered over the rough veld track in a mood of depression. A family of little meerkats sat up to pray, their tiny paws on their chests. They made him think of miniature kangaroos in the Australian dusk, frozen and inquisitive. Over the rise the lights of Pierre's house were homely and inviting in the great emptiness of the veld. The night wind was bitterly cold.

A Bantu groom took Star from him as he dismounted, and led the stallion towards the stables. Franz went up to the front door and Zirelda Malan opened it for him.

'Come in out of the cold,' she said in Afrikaans. 'It's nice to see you.'

Behind her, in the living-room, a young girl rose shyly from her place on the old fashioned fender that enclosed the open hearth where a log fire blazed with noisy spluttering. She was quite a big girl – seventeen, perhaps – with a round childish face, large gentian blue eyes and corn coloured hair that streamed over her shoulders, straight as pump water.

'My young sister, Hortense Malherbe,' said Zirelda. 'She's staying with us for a while. Hortense, this is Franz Morley.'

He put out his hand. 'I'm glad to meet you, Hortense.'

Her hand was surprisingly small and soft, and, when she smiled, she dimpled.

'Hallo, Franz,' her voice was soft too.

'School holidays?' he asked.

Her eyes twinkled. 'I've finished school. When I go back to Benoni I mean to get myself a job.'

'As what?'

'I don't know yet. I'll think about it while I'm here.'

'Brandy, or sherry?' Pierre asked Franz. 'Or beer?'

'Beer, please.'

Hortense had resumed her place on the leather seat of the fender. The flames added to the glow of her healthy complexion and turned her hair to liquid gold. Her profile was towards the fire, blunt and malleable like a child's, but the line of her chin curving into her smooth rounded neck was firm and womanly, so was the high bosom under her blouse. She was wearing slacks and he could not judge her legs, but her ankles were neat.

'Do you play tennis?' he asked.

'Yes,' she said. 'I love it. Zirelda says you have a splendid court.'

'Quite a good one. You must come over and we'll play some singles.'

'Oh, yes, let's!'

She wasn't arch. She didn't say, 'Oh, but you'll be too good for me.' She simply assumed that she could give him a game.

He looked at Hortense with her child's face, her soft hands and her woman's pretty throat, and he decided that he liked her very much.

In the weeks that followed Hortense Malherbe fell into the habit of going over to Golden Grass to play tennis with Franz. In fact, she had no need to be modest about her game, for she was a steady and forceful player, and, as often as not, she beat him. Sometimes she rode over in her old corduroy slacks and light wool jersey with her long hair streaming out like her pony's tail in the spring sunshine. At others she borrowed her sister's car. Occasionally Pierre and Zirelda came too and played against Franz and Hortense in a well contested four.

Dave's message came one evening when Franz and Hortense had just finished a game. They were sitting in the sun-porch when the telephone rang. Her white tennis dress was as brief as a ballerina's tutu and her bare legs were curled up under her in the big easy chair. A long lemon squash, as yet untouched, was on the small stinkwood table beside her. Her blue cardigan hung loosely across her shoulders. She had driven over in Zirelda's car and brought a change. Franz had suggested she stay for supper and the idea seemed good to her. Hortense, for all her schoolgirl appearance, was very much a woman, and lately she had admitted to herself that she was mad about Franz.

He went through into the living-room and she heard him take up the receiver and talk to the exchange in quick anxious Afrikaans. He called to her.

'I have to hang on. It's a Cape call – my brother Dave.'

'Shall I make myself scarce?'

'Why should you? It's a party line.'

But she uncoiled her limbs reluctantly and went to his desk by the sliding landscape window. She took up the framed snapshot on it. A girl with a gay laughing face and short dark hair looked back at her. The girl wore a white bikini and her body and limbs were beautiful. Once Hortense had asked Franz about her.

'She's Australian,' he had said briefly.

'Unfinished business?'

'Finished business,' he had answered, and his voice had put an end to her probing. Yet, if it were really finished, this snapshot would hardly be there on his desk. She put it down and shivered, for the evening was still cold. The patchwork lands were rosy in the setting sun. The caller might take some time to come through. A hot shower, woollen slacks and a turtle necked pullover would be more to the point than her tennis dress. Her legs and thighs were beginning to get mottled from the cold. Really, they weren't her best feature. Not like the Australian girl's. She went into the living-room.

'I'm going to change, Franz. I know my way to your spare room.'

'Do that,' he said. And to the exchange: 'Ja, goed . . .'

Her tennis shoes made no sound as she pattered down the long passage and then Franz heard the shower and a sudden picture of the fair skinned body of Hortense under the needles of hot water invaded his mind. He saw her as if through steam, her long hair pinned up on top of her head. He almost smelled the warmth of her young soapy flesh. What the hell did Dave want with him? They weren't in the habit of telephoning long distance. It must be some emergency. His brother's voice came on the line and Franz knew at once that something was seriously amiss.

'It's Mum,' Dave was saying. 'She's terribly ill and she's asking for you. Can you get a plane tonight?'

Franz glanced at the clock over the mantelpiece. Not yet six o'clock.

'Yes. I can just make it. What about Kevin?'

'Jules is phoning Kevin right now. He'll certainly make one of tonight's flights.'

'So will I. What's wrong with Mum?' He tried to keep his voice steady.

'It's inoperable cancer, Franz. She's known for months and refused to have us – or anyone – told. Now there's a sudden deterioration.'

In that horrible agonizing moment of realization Franz knew what he had tried not to face – that he had really come home to see his mother before she died. Dave said:

'The Old Man's taking it hard. He needs us all.'

'We'll be with him. I'll ring or wire you from the airport. Give her my love, Dave . . . tell her I'm on my way . . .'

He put down the receiver and buried his face in his hands. As he raised it he saw the girl in her slacks and pullover, her long fair hair damp from the shower, her eyes questioning. She put her warm hand to his cheek.

'What is it?'

'My mother is dying.'

Her eyes reflected the shock in his.

'You must go to her at once?'

'At once.'

'Of course. God bless you, Franz.'

Her arms wound about his neck and she was offering her soft childish lips. He kissed her without passion and put her gently from him.

'I'm sorry, Tennie,' he said.

'I hope it won't be as bad as you fear. Is there any way I can help?'

'None, my dear. I must pack a few things and be on my way.'

'Then I'll go home. Goodbye, Franz.'

'I'll come to the car with you.'

She drove back to her sister's home under the koppie across the veld. When she ran the car into the shed the light was fading fast. Her brother-in-law was there, tinkering with the tractor. He glanced at her face, drained of its usual healthy colour.

'What's up, Tennie?'

She told him. They spoke in Afrikaans.

He wiped his hands on some cotton waste and closed the tool case he'd been using. Then he flung a brawny arm around her shoulder.

'So now he goes and leaves you. That's life, Sussie. Like my bloody tractor here. It's full of loose ends and uncertainties. It may limp along tomorrow or it may not with that pumpkin, Dagbreek, at the wheel —'

'It's your own fault with the tractor,' she said severely. 'You know quite well there isn't a native living who will bother with servicing a machine. He drives it till it falls apart, whether it's Dagbreek or any of his relatives.'

'Ja, I know. And I know that tonight you will cry for Franz.'

'I won't cry,' she said hotly. 'Hey, keep your hands to yourself, Boetie!'

Pierre chuckled. 'I like having you around.'

'Well then, pas op! My sister, Zirelda, has never shared her toys with me.' She stalked out of the shed, haughty, desirable and defensive. He caught up with her and linked his arm in hers. They strolled down the path towards the house. He was fond of his sister-in-law and liked to tease her and he was well aware that his neighbour was a catch for any girl not dazzled by city lights. It would be nice too for Zirelda to have Tennie just over the rise a few miles away.

'You know I'm always thinking for your good,' he said. 'You must stay with us till Franz gets back. After that ons kan 'n plan maak.'

Her lip curled. 'Make a plan and everything'll come right. Alles sal reg kom. Not so?'

'Just so.'

'You know something,' she said. 'Franz has got some unfinished business in Australia. He keeps her picture on his desk, a girl in a bikini.'

'Ag, that's just a pin-up. I'll bet she's not as pretty as you.'

She reflected. 'Better legs, longer, thinner. An interesting face with short dark hair. Not a pudding like mine. He won't talk about her.'

'She's a long way off. You're here – right on the spot.'

She smiled, cheered by his man's philosophy. But she said, 'I'd do best to go back to Benoni and find myself a job.'

'If you've got to pick between the job and the man, you should go for the man – this particular man. You're no career girl.'

'I'm seventeen,' she said. 'I need experience —'

'So what am I for?'

She laughed and broke away from him and began to run in the direction of the house. It was nearly dark and the scent of the freshly ploughed earth mounted to her nostrils, the windmill clonked in the evening silence and she took great gulps of the frosty highveld air. She felt keenly wonderfully alive, as if her energy were overflowing, leaving a bright *spoor*, glowing round her swift figure like a will-o'-the-wisp aura. The more she thought about Franz's mother dying away down there at the Cape the more she felt the power of her own life force, its demands, fierce and subtle, its potent magic making her one with the vast uplands, with every living creature, with the past and the future, with the lover she desired and the children latent in her urgently awakened body. She could smell the dew on the grass at the side of the path – wild unkempt grass. In the early morning there'd be spiders' webs across it glistening with rime. She heard Pierre at her heels, his long limber stride. He'd been a fine runner at school – a stayer. Then he was a step ahead of her, opening the garden gate and they were walking sedately through the vegetable patch with its marrows and tomatoes, its rows of peas, beans, feathery carrot leaves and squat cabbages, reducing the whole vast highveld to the limits of a woman's kitchen.

'You certainly can sprint,' said Pierre. 'Were you running away from me?'

'You flatter yourself. I was running to ... towards ...' She broke off uncertain of what she really wanted to express.

'Towards life?'

'Oh, just running for the hell of it,' she shrugged. 'Just because it's good to be seventeen and not an old lady with her family gathering round her deathbed – that sort of thing.'

'Ja,' he said. 'I understand.'

On the other side of the rise, Franz, alone in his car on the darkening veld, put his foot down heavily on the accelerator. He'd just about make the airport in time for the last night flight to Cape Town.

For once Storm looked tired and overwrought. She pulled off her small black hat and shook her hair free so that it tossed buoyantly on the shoulders of her grey dress. She dragged off her gloves and ran her fingers through her flattened red-gold mane, pushing it up.

'Damn hats!' she said. 'That going back to tea at Blue Horizon after the cremation was a nightmare. A family gathering with *her* not there . . .' She shuddered. 'And the Old Man looking so terrible – blank and numb and a thousand years old.'

'He did his best,' said Dave. 'But he was like a sleep-walker.'

'And in the church,' she grumbled. 'Elijah and Lettie – to say nothing of the cowherd and that half-witted gardener – all in deepest mourning, snivelling down our necks in the pew directly behind ours. It was enough to upset anybody. Even Lettie's gloves were black.'

Both outwardly and inwardly Lettie mourned my mother more sincerely than you did, thought Dave, as he followed her into the living-room. Rain streamed against the window panes and it was bitterly cold for September, more like winter than spring. He bent and put a match to the fire. It flared into life at once and the stacked fir cones glowed and crackled with yellow and violet lights. The children scampered into the room, Gaby holding little Garth's hand.

'Not this evening,' said Storm sharply. 'We can't play with you this evening. Phoebe must put you to bed.' She called Phoebe and told her to take the children to the nursery and read to them. 'We'll come up later and kiss them goodnight,' she added.

Dave patted their heads absently, and crestfallen and protesting, they allowed themselves to be led away.

Moses, the butler, brought a tray of glasses, minerals and

ice and placed it on the table next to the locked corner
cupboard where Dave kept his drinks. Dave detested locking
anything away but it wasn't fair to leave temptation under
Moses' nose. The young coloured man was the descendant
of generations of labourers in the Cape vineyards who had
been paid for their toil in part by the wine of the grapes
they tended. Thus the craving for a 'doppie' had long since
been bred into their systems. It was part of a cruel heritage
– that and the white blood that put them into a twilight
world between the pure bred Bantu and the European
baas-men who ruled their land. Yet they got their own
back every now and again when a crimpy-haired dark-
skinned child was born to some white family with an old
proud name.

Storm sank into an easy chair. 'A whisky, Dave. Make it
strong.'

He unlocked the cupboard and poured her drink and his
own. He lit a cigarette for each of them and then began to
pace up and down the room.

'Don't do that!' she cried suddenly. 'It gets on my nerves.'

'I have nerves too.' But he sat down opposite her and took
a gulp of his whisky.

'Magda and Jules, Kevin and Colleen, Franz – the whole
clan here,' she said. 'But tomorrow your brothers go back
up-country and the Old Man will have to face life at Blue
Horizon on his own.'

'When things are settled here he'll go to Franz for a while.
He's interested in the farm. It'll do him good.'

'After that will he go on living at Blue Horizon?'

'I think so. It's early to know. But my guess is that he
will.'

'Yes, he has to be the pivot – the kingpin. We'll all have to kowtow to him. He'll expect Phoebe to take the kids over daily as usual to see the Big Boss. If he wants the kids all that much why the devil can't they stay there with him while we go away for a holiday trip. Italy, Greece, a Mediterranean tour, a change and some fun.'

Her voice was bitter. Of late she had been increasingly belligerent, bored with domesticity and life in Somerset West. She wanted to travel and she expected the Old Man to pay up.

'Why shouldn't he give us a jaunt overseas?' she reverted to the subject closest to her heart. 'I could do with a rest from this dead-and-alive hole and the Morley clique. I want to see new places, meet new people, buy new clothes, enjoy myself. When I married you I thought we'd see something of the world, spend some of that Morley fortune —'

'And you got a poor bargain! You got me – without my father's fortune.'

'So right!'

He turned his haggard face to her, drawn with grief for his mother, tense with the failure of his marriage – for failure he now knew it to be. He spoke to her through tight lips, biting off his words.

'There was a wreath without a message or a name on my mother's coffin today. White and mauve everlastings, white roses and a satin bow – the facsimile of the wreath Magda received when young Hector was born. You sent it. Deny it, if you can!'

'I sent the wreath to your mother. It was my personal tribute. Why should you object?' Her tone was contemptuous and defiant.

'Why indeed – if Magda had not been sent just such a symbol of death to celebrate the birth of her child? Did you try to put a spell on our family then? A death wish for somebody near and dear? If so, you certainly succeeded.'

She gave a short ugly laugh. 'You almost believe that, don't you? Evil eye stuff.' But although she spoke with sarcastic contempt a red light flickered in her consciousness, a warning that the intensity of her own sinister impulses was dangerous to her as well as to others. It was as if she approached a traffic signal without brakes. If she didn't exert some control soon more people were going to get hurt. She too perhaps.

'You *do* wish death on people!' said Dave. 'My father, for instance.'

She got up and helped herself to a second whisky stronger than the one he'd given her. She was coldly angry. Why couldn't he leave her to indulge her own gimmicks in her own way?

'Aren't you getting rather hot under the collar about nothing?'

She was on the arm of the chair now, not settled, ready for a move either way, waiting for something to develop. For what? Her face was watchful, her upper lip drawn back from her teeth in a grimace that was half a smile, half snarl, daring him to speak his mind openly.

'Did you send Sidney Barralet a wreath like that? Everlastings and white roses? Your emblem.'

'Flowers from a gangster to a victim. Is that what you're suggesting? You've had that in the back of your mind for a long time, haven't you?'

'For an eternity,' he said wearily. 'I think I guessed at the very beginning but I wouldn't believe anything so terrible. Sometimes when I saw you with Gaby, your cruelty – hiding her beloved doll to punish her for some trifle – it rose up like vomit in my throat – this horrible suspicion, this wondering what you were capable of –'

'What am I capable of?' Her eyes were mere slits, her lips compressed.

'Murder,' he said in a low voice.

'You think I'll admit that?'

'How did you do it?'

She threw back her head and laughed in a shrill frightening way as if at some macabre jest no one could share. He got up and went to her, his dark eyes smouldering. He slapped her cheek with the palm of his open hand.

'Shut up! You're laughing like a mad woman.'

She choked on her own hysterical laughter and sprang to her feet, gasping.

'How did I do it? I did nothing – absolutely nothing.'

She saw again the thin imploring paper-pale face, and heard the frantic entreaties. His tablets? Where were his tablets?

'Nothing, nothing, nothing,' she repeated.

'I don't believe you.'

'A game of hide-and-seek, perhaps, like I play with Gaby when I punish her by hiding her doll where she can't find it. Hide-and-seek can be a fatal game.'

'So you did that! You hid his tablets!'

'For love – for money – one will do a great deal.'

He seized her shoulders and shook her, hating himself and hating her. He flung her away from him and she almost fell but recovered herself and faced him, her fists clenched.

'Did you really never guess? Or did you know all along? Maybe it suited you to be blind. Then open your eyes now and see me as I am! I don't maim and kill people with my own hands but I set the stage and the rest follows. What is to be will be.'

He turned his back on her and she saw his shoulders stoop as his father's had stooped at the church. She heard his voice, clipped and horrified, as he bit off the words.

'You're wicked. You're sinful. I'll never live with you again as your husband.'

'And I'll never give you your freedom. You'll never be shot of me, Dave Morley.'

'You're a devil – a fiend.'

'Then you've lost your soul to the devil. So make the best of it.'

He did what he always did when she tormented him. He turned and left her as if the sight of her sickened him. She heard the car start up and knew that he had gone up into the woods regardless of the storm, that he would walk in the hills and heatherlands until he was exhausted, that he would come back hours later, drenched to the skin, and go to the spare-room. For days afterwards he would look like a man doomed – silent, depressed, wearing a polite mask when he faced Hettie Conradie, his secretary, who knew his moods so well. He'd play with the children automatically, lifelessly, and he would ignore Storm until she forced him into some sign of recognition.

But tonight – the night of his mother's funeral – was different for Dave. This time he knew that he could never again resume his life with Storm. The intangible horror that had haunted him for months, the unspeakable suspicion, had materialized at last and he knew his wife for what she was – a scheming pitiless woman who would stop at nothing to get what she wanted. That she had wanted him, Dave, and had loved him after her fashion, did not minimize his revulsion. It only added to his sense of guilt. But for him, she might have let nature take its course with Sidney Barralet. He must get away or one day there would be another tragedy. He had indeed lost his soul to the devil and only by escape could he hope to save it.

Three days later he went to see his father. Kevin, Colleen and Franz had already returned to the Transvaal, and Blue Horizon was sadly lonely without them and without its gentle mistress. However, the Old Man had planned to go and stay with Franz for a while and it was his intention to fly north the following day. He received his son in his study. Lettie had put a few flowers on the desk in an effort to brighten up the room. Dave looked into his father's pain-filled eyes and thought that he really was an old man now, bowed and broken by his loss.

'Dad,' said Dave. 'I want to see you on a personal matter. I need your help and advice.'

Hector Morley hauled himself out of the abyss of his own suffering to confront his son's trouble. Dave looked dreadful. The past eighteen months had transformed him from a gay young blood to a man steeped in deep disillusion. The despair on his face alarmed his father. Hector sat in his old leather arm-chair and Dave sat opposite him and lit a cigarette. The young man's fingers were nicotine stained and one hand stroked the mahogany surface of the desk, running up and down the faded gilt border that divided hand-polished wood from time-worn hide.

'It's Storm,' he said. The Old Man waited in silence. Sooner or later he had expected some confidence of this sort.

'I can't go on with her,' Dave burst out. 'I've found things out . . . things I simply cannot take.'

'What things?'

'I'd rather not say.'

'If I'm to help you I must know everything.'

The Old Man lit his pipe and puffed smoke rings into the air. A sunbeam caught them and they were dispersed in the slight draught coming in through the open window. A bird sang in the garden, the complicated trills and arpeggios of the spring.

'That business about the wreaths —'

'When Magda's son was born?'

Dave nodded. 'She was responsible.'

'What else?'

'Her husband – old Sidney Barralet – had a bad heart. She . . . I can't . . .'

'You must.'

'He needed certain tablets. They were vital. She hid them.'

Dave buried his face in his hands. His cigarette burned slowly on the edge of the ashtray and after a while the Old Man leaned forward and stubbed it out.

'Murder by default,' he said with no particular surprise. 'And she probably told him about you at the same time – just to build up the tension in him.'

'I never thought of that. It makes me an accessory.'

'Hardly. But a woman as unscrupulous as Storm stops at nothing. She's clever too. No one can prove anything. A sick man has died, the tablets are back in their place, his time had come anyway and the doctor had no misgivings. When did you learn these things?'

'Last night I knew for certain. I'd suspected before but I wouldn't admit it to myself.'

'So now —?'

Dave flung back his head. 'So now I must get away – desert her. I can't live with Storm after this and survive.'

'She won't let you go. She wants your money, and your ultimate share of mine – which she'll never get.'

'When she fully realizes that she'll let me go.'

'At a price.'

'I'll meet that situation when it arises. At present I only know one thing, I must get away from her – as far as possible. I may become a wanderer. No one must know where I am.'

'What about the firm?' said the Old Man tersely. 'You seem to be considering only yourself.'

'The firm doesn't really need me. Hettie Conradie knows more about the business side than I do and any surveyor could take my place. They don't need a geologist.'

'But you happen to need the firm. You are paid a salary.'

'I'll find a job wherever I go.'

'You'll have to support your wife and children while you're looking for it.'

'I'll draw on my capital to do that.'

The Old Man's jaw tightened. 'I've always told you never to live on capital.'

'Then help me with a loan.'

'I shall expect interest.'

'Of course.'

'Storm will try to get in touch with you.'

'She can do so through my lawyer – Warren Keller. I'll let him – and you – know where I am, in absolute confidence.'

'Not me. I'm the keeper of no man's secrets.'

'Will you help me with the loan? Will you make it possible for me to clear out?'

'Before I answer that question I have another to ask you.'

The Old Man's pipe had gone out and he relit it. Dave waited.

'Have you considered the children?'

'Yes,' Dave said. 'I've given them some thought —'

'*Some* thought is not enough!'

'Dad, look, even Storm – even she – wouldn't harm her own children. She adores Garth —'

'And Gaby?'

'She wouldn't hurt Gaby – not in any physical sense. A smack with a hairbrush now and again. Nothing worse. And you and Magda and Jules could keep an eye on them for me.'

'But eventually? If you make it possible for her to divorce you – practically force her to – how can you claim the children?'

'I've thought of that.'

'Well?'

'I can buy her off – buy my own son, and Gaby into the bargain.'

'You mean *I* can – if she's willing to sell.'

'Will you?'

'I don't know, Dave. I don't know if you're a fit person to have the custody of children.'

'You know *she* isn't.'

'She really loves Garth. She may refuse.'

'Can we let that problem solve itself – later.'

'Problems of this magnitude don't usually solve themselves but yes, we can let it ride – if you trust her not to hurt
those children in the meantime. Can you give me that
absolute assurance?'

Dave rose and went to the window. He inhaled the fresh
sunny air. He looked into his own heart and found it shallow
and full of uncertainties. He ignored them as he said:

'I can give you that assurance. Even she —'

'Don't weaken your case, my boy. I asked for your
assurance not your opinion. You know the children and you
know the mother. You know if you feel justified in shaking
off the responsibility and leaving them to her tender mercies.
I have to trust your judgement.'

Dave had his back to his father. I don't know, damn it, he
thought. How the devil can I believe in Storm's maternal
instinct when my trust in everything about her is in frag-
ments? I'm only certain of one thing. I must get out or go
mad. I know what she's done, and, though she may be able
to live with it, I can't! The children don't know. They're
defenceless. I'll have to hope they'll be all right because they
are hers – her own. Anyway, there's Dad. There's Mag.
There's Phoebe, who loves them. He turned to his father.

'I feel justified in leaving them. It'll only be for a while.
A few months at most. Storm's hot blooded. Someone will
take my place and then she'll want her freedom.'

'Then get hold of Warren Keller. We'll see him in his
chambers. Today if possible. No one must know anything
about this. Not Kevin or Franz or Magda. No one, except
you and me – and I refuse to be told where you're going. Is
that understood?'

The Old Man rose. His back was straight once more, his lips were firm. He put his great hands on the young man's shoulders.

'It's a bad business. I'm sorry.'

Dave looked at his father with his sad hollow black eyes.

'Thank you, Dad. Most of all, thank you for not saying "I told you so".'

A ghost of a smile flickered over Hector Morley's features. He felt that he had won a long battle.

'And, Dad, for God's sake be careful. She's vengeful and she hates you. She's dangerous.'

'I know she's dangerous,' said the Old Man. 'That's why I'm helping you. This is a rescue operation. It's not too late.'

7

DANGEROUS FRIENDSHIP

PHILIPPA LEANED CLOSER TO THE LOOKING-GLASS TO submit her face to one of those long critical inspections women inflict upon themselves before going to a cocktail party. Her skin after the rainy Perth winter, was clear and soft, denuded of its summer tan and her eyes were bright but they held a certain discontent which could only be dispelled by an effort of will. Soon after Franz's departure Mrs Collins had undergone a serious operation and Phil had felt compelled to give up her job and live at home to look after her parents. There! she had thought, just imagine how I'd have felt if I'd gone to South Africa with Franz! Yet physically and emotionally she ached for him still.

'Pull yourself together,' she told the mirror image firmly. 'What you need is a boyfriend, my girl. It's ten months since Franz left.'

She added a final dab of powder and a touch of lipstick and slipped on a gaudy woolly jacket over her short blue dress. Ian Gray had given it to her for Christmas. It was made of Australian wool and designed by a famous fashion house in Melbourne and she knew that it suited her. She went in to her mother's room. Mrs Collins was dressed but was resting on her bed as she often did in the evening before her husband's return. She looked up and smiled at Phil.

'You look enchanting.'

Phil laughed. 'The eye of the beholder. See you later, Mom – though, come to that, I may not. You know what cocktail parties are like —'

'Apt to go on till midnight. Have you got your key? You know, darling, I wish you weren't going alone. Can't you get a lift – or give one?'

'I prefer to be independent. If you get a lift you have to stay late or leave early to suit the person you go with. I'd rather suit myself.'

'But it's quite a long way – right the other side of Perth.'

'Five minutes or twenty – what's it matter? Don't worry. Kiss Pop goodnight for me.'

Her heart lifted as she let herself out of the house. Her mother certainly looked much better. Maybe later it would be possible to resume her teaching. But the thought of Broken Hill, of Black Swan and the Menindee Lakes sent a red-hot arrow into her. Broken Hill could never be the same again for her. Better to take a job here in Perth where there were no ghosts to haunt her. Or Adelaide perhaps!

She parked the Holden on the grass verge outside the house in a valley of vineyards. The party was already in full swing. Most of the guests ringed around in the long living-room, others, less susceptible to the evening's chill, had spilled over onto the terrace where the bar was set up. The host was her father's lawyer, Geoffrey Grace. Janet Grace greeted Phil warmly.

'Can we expect your father later?'

'I doubt it,' said Phil. 'He practically never goes to cocktail parties.'

Mrs Grace looked vaguely round. 'Oh, dear, what a pity. But I know how it is. How's your mother?'

'Doing fine.'

'That's good. Here's Geoff. He'll get you a drink.'

Janet evaporated among her guests and left Geoff with Philippa.

'What'll it be?' he asked.

'Gin and tonic,' she said. 'I'll come with you onto the terrace, Geoff.'

She followed his tubby figure and bald head through the French doors. Clusters of coloured bulbs hung among the pergola of vine leaves, pretending to be grapes, and shafts of brighter light spilled onto the tiles through the open door of the main room. She sat on a low stone parapet while Geoff fetched her a drink.

'Have a cushion,' said a girl next to her, 'or you'll get you know what.'

Phil laughed and accepted the proffered cushion. The girl had turned back to her companion and Phil looked round to see who she knew. Almost everybody. Suddenly she withdrew into the shadow, flattening herself against the pillar. Her heart was pounding and her palms tingled. There – over there – talking to Janet Grace was . . . no, it couldn't be! How could it? His back was to her, tall, broad shouldered, the head set in that unmistakable familiar fashion. The shape of it, the stance, the whole silhouette could be only one person. He'd come back to fetch her! Impossible. He would have come over to her at once.

'You all right?'

Geoff was standing over her with a glass in his hand.

'Sure,' she said, accepting the drink and shaking off the moment of hallucination. But her eyes were still riveted by the tall figure in the half light. He had turned and she saw his profile. High-bridged hawk nose, springing hair, but dark not fair like Franz's. He was using his hands to illustrate a point – long tapering fingers. For the first time in her life everything in her whole being seemed to falter.

Geoff said: 'Oh, by the way, I must bring a stranger along to meet you. He's from Cape Town. He knows your father. He's over there, talking to Janet.'

Before she could stop him he had left her and within seconds he was returning to her side with the stranger who moved with the easy subtle grace that she remembered so well.

'Phil,' he said. 'Meet Mr Davis from Cape Town, South Africa. Miss Philippa Collins.'

She rose and was acutely aware that if he were to take her in his arms her head would be under his chin – the chin slightly cleft just as she had guessed it would be. His dark stranger's eyes looked into hers, and although their shape and colour was Franz's, their expression was far different. These were eyes without faith set in the haggard face of a young man who had lost the the essence of youth. A shiver ran through her.

'Philippa Collins,' he repeated, and suddenly he smiled. 'I've met your father.'

'And you?' she said, her voice taut. 'What is your other name, Mr Davis?'

'My other name?' His smile vanished and for a moment he seemed at a loss. His voice was deeper than Franz's, less mellow.

'Your first name? Or must I be formal and call you Mr Davis?'

'My first name is my guilty secret, Philippa. Or is it Phil?'

'Phil.'

'Who wouldn't hide a name like Horatio? People call me Dave.'

'I see . . . Dave. You wouldn't by any chance know a friend of mine in South Africa – Franz Morley?'

He looked down at her, deadpan.

'Sorry.'

'I knew him rather well,' she said.

'Lucky devil.'

'When did you arrive in Perth?'

'Yesterday.'

'And when did you meet my father?'

'This morning. A chap on the plane gave me an introduction. He said there were fantastic things going on in the north-west – iron ore discoveries that would bring a whole new world into being, change Western Australia from the Cinderella state into the hub of the Commonwealth. He said the discovery had launched a vast immigration scheme and that your father was the driving force behind the whole development. I'm a gambler by nature and I smell fortunes to be made in the north-west.'

'You were well informed,' she said drily. 'There's room for all in the vacuum of the north-west. But you've got to be tough.'

'Don't you think I'm tough?'

'How would I know?'

'How indeed? Mr Grace was with your father when I called on him and he asked me to come to this party. That's a welcoming example of Australian hospitality. I'm hoping your father may find me a job.'

'What sort of job?'

'I'm a surveyor and a geologist.'

'He might be able to use someone like that,' she said thoughtfully. 'But you'd find it hard going in the outback. The iron ore country is hundreds of miles from here – a hot, lonely, unexploited territory. I doubt if it would be up your street.'

'It would be up my street all right. Where I come from my street is a cul-de-sac – the sort of street that has an Afrikaans notice at the entrance, Straat Loop Dood. Street walks dead. You reach an end. You have to stop and start again.' He spoke bitterly and, as she watched his face, the likeness to Franz seemed ephemeral, yet, when he smiled, it was there again.

Somebody had started up a record player and one or two couples were already dancing. Dave looked down at Philippa with that quick heart-catching grin.

'Shall we dance?'

For a moment she hesitated. The tune was one she associated with Franz. But, inevitably, she moved forward into Dave's arms.

Janet Grace had prepared a cold fork buffet for those who wanted to stay on to supper and it was near midnight before the guests began to drift away. She bustled over to where Phil was taking leave of Geoff. Janet was flushed with the success of her party and with the wine. She had noticed the preoccupation of the stranger with Phil Collins, and it amused her to encourage it. Phil had been very aloof of late. She was one of the few young women who refused to be monopolised by any one man.

'Oh, darling,' Janet said. 'Mr Davis' hotel is practically on your way home. Could you give him a lift?'

'Of course – if he's ready to come now.'

The night was cool, and before long they were crossing the causeway and driving along the river bank with Perth on their right and up on the hill the forests of King's Park dark and sweet smelling in the late spring. The wide Swan River reflected the wavering lights of softly swaying boats and graceful bridges and the silver pinpoints of high southern stars.

'When am I going to see you again?' Dave asked.

'When are you seeing my father?'

'Tomorrow – or should I say today? In a few hours time.'

'We'd better wait till after that.'

'I want to see you anyway.'

'You can ring me up when you've talked to Pop.'

'Will you put in a word for me?'

'No, I will not, Mr Davis. I know nothing whatever about you.'

He flushed in the green deathly light of the street lamps as she goaded him, her tone mocking.

'You're a man without a past or a future, as far as I am concerned. Have you a wife and children? Do you mean to make a home for them in this continent? Or are you free to do as you like, go where you like, fall in love with who-ever you like? Who are you really, Mr Horatio Davis? There's something of the Flying Dutchman about you – a haunted feeling.'

She thought suddenly that the wine had been more potent than she'd realized. She slowed down, attentive to the road, intensely aware of the man at her side, this man so like Franz who was called Dave, the name of Franz's brother who had married a woman his family hated and feared.

'You're very sensitive,' he said quietly. 'Very sensible too. Why should you trust a stranger with a haunted look about him?' He laughed without mirth. 'I hope your father will be less fey.'

'My father will judge for himself. His standards are based on competence – and liking, of course.'

'And yours?'

'On liking – and instinct.'

'Do you find me difficult to like?'

'I find you very secretive – Dave.'

'That's no answer to my question.'

'You don't answer many questions yourself.'

'Touché,' he agreed. 'Not everybody can tell his life story to a stranger, however fascinating he may find her.'

She felt a tremor pass through her nerves. They say women always fall for the same type of man. There was this strong likeness between Dave and Franz to confuse her senses and yet he was utterly different. Bolder, more selfish, she guessed, infinitely more worldly. She was very conscious of his physical attraction. I'm in that sort of mood, she thought. Careful, now!

She turned the car up and away from the river, crossing the highway at the traffic lights. She drove through a gateway and drew up in the scented shade of a tall magnolia.

'Here we are, stranger. Your hotel. It seems to be asleep.'

She left the engine running. She had promised nothing for tomorrow or any other day, but she was quivering and afraid that he might feel the vibration of her body although they were not touching. Dave leaned forward and switched off the ignition.

'So it's you,' he said. 'It's you trembling. Why?'

He slid his arm along the seat behind her and drew her to him, shaken by his knowledge of her awakened senses, by her softness and firmness under his hands. He longed to talk to her, to confide in her, to make love to her. But she stiffened and pushed him away.

'Go, now,' she said through dry lips. 'Go, Dave.'

'Phil, we'll have to meet again.'

'Ring me tomorrow – after you've seen my father.'

He dragged himself from her against every instinct of mind and body. This Phil Collins whose name he had heard from Franz, had she really been Franz's girl? He had written about her often enough but after his return to South Africa he had seldom mentioned her and the family had been led to believe that there was 'nothing in it'. More fool Franz!

'Goodnight, Phil.'

She heard the door slam and saw him standing in the shadow of the tree. He watched the car move and turn in front of the hotel and presently the red rear light disappeared into the night to merge with the late traffic of the Highway.

Phil opened her curtains before getting into bed. She stood gazing at the river, breathing the cool night air, trying to clear her mind of its confusion.

She put out the light and lay sleepless, wondering and guessing. Franz and she had agreed not to write to one another. She had insisted that the break should be complete, and now here was this mysterious South African who so closely resembled Franz. Surely he must be Dave Morley. People's names were themselves, symbols of their identity. Even criminals hated giving up their own names and clung to some vestige or anagram of the original in creating an alias. Davis – Dave. Did he know about her? Had Franz talked about her? Had Dave heard about Mr Collins and the north-west from Franz or from the acquaintance in the plane? Both perhaps. Was he escaping from something or someone? If so, what and who? What should she do? Confront him with her guess that he was Franz's brother or play it his way and accept him as a stranger? There were many like him in Australia – always had been – men determined to make a new start. They came to the Far Country, hope overriding past failures, and the majority won through. No ghosts here – except those within them – to haunt their daily lives. Their surroundings were totally unfamiliar and even their work was often different from anything they had ever done before. Had Franz's brother become one of their number – one of these exiles? She moved restlessly, tingling with the hunger Dave had wakened in her. Hunger for Franz or for Dave? She hardly knew. She sensed in this stranger knowledge of passion – you couldn't call it love – very different from his brother's. At last, when the stars paled, she fell asleep.

She had just returned from her morning marketing when her father telephoned her from the office.

'Phil, I'll be bringing a young man home to dinner this evening. Name of Davis. He's a South African but he doesn't know our friend Franz Morley, though, oddly enough, he has a look of Franz.'

'I met him last night, Pop. At the Graces.'

'So he told me. He doesn't know many people here as yet, and I may be giving him a job. He's flying with me to Hamersley the day after tomorrow.'

'How did he manage to get in touch with you?'

Mr Collins laughed. 'South Africans read newspapers like

everybody else. Western Australia's iron ore – the world's richest deposits – have been front page news for quite a while and this guy's a surveyor and a geologist. O'Connor was on the plane with him and gave him an introduction to me. He might be useful. We'll be home around six o'clock.'

Phil put down the receiver thoughtfully. She had the feeling of being on strings. A dancing puppet. What mocking force was the puppeteer?

It was Mrs Collins who made the suggestion at dinner.

'Why don't you fly to Hamersley with Pop and Dave, Phil?' He was Dave to her parents already. 'Aunt Evelyn'll keep me company. You'll only be away for two or three days.'

'Thirty six hours,' said Mr Collins. 'I have to get back here for a meeting. And I propose to leave Dave on the station with Vic Craig, if he decides he can take life in the raw.'

So the three of them flew by the M.M.A. Fokker Friendship from Perth airport before dawn on a chill spring morning. By sunrise they were high above the empty bush country, red earth hazed over with the prickly grey-blue spinifex, the scourge of human or animal feet, and a few hundred miles later the long horsehoe of the mineral bearing Hamersleys ridged the salmon coloured landscape in convolutions of unbelievable lavenders, crimsons and the dark indigo of deep canyons. Here, north of the twenty-sixth Parallel, they were in the red heart of the north-west, a lonely frontier land that Jim Collins envisaged coming to healthy, wealthy life with mining and railway towns and the international immigration of thousands of new Australians.

The sun was high in the sky when they came down at the

small outback asbestos town of Wittenoom and within moments they had left the Fokker Friendship airliner and were walking over to Mr Collins' private four-seater single-engined Cessna.

'Victor Craig, my station manager – Mr Davis – Dave to his friends,' Mr Collins introduced the young man who had piloted the Cessna. Craig smiled widely. He was sandy-haired, stocky and robust. Little bush flies clustered over the back of his khaki shirt, he was used to them and ignored them. They were part of the country like the weather that soared to 120° in the height of summer. As they took their places, Mr Collins said:

'Dave's from South Africa – a surveyor and geologist. I want him to have a look round our territory.'

Soon they were flying into the crescent of the Hamersleys and Craig swooped down to show Dave the iron clad bastions yielding the vast quantities of ore that was railed to the new harbours already prepared to take the fleet of ships needed to transport the ore to Japan and to other lands.

'It's there,' he said. 'External, as you see, asking to be mined and exported. Two million acres of land below you belonged to me formerly. I used to run sheep on one half and cattle on the other. I still do on the land I've kept. We need meat for the mining towns that are literally springing up while you watch. It's a tremendous project. Some of the mineral samples in these mountains would make your eyes bulge. Here we are now – just coming down over the station.

They saw the usual windmills and mobs of cattle in the shade of trees growing near the water. A flock of white cockatoos rose into the air like flowers blowing away in a gale. Then they were circling over a large single-storeyed house surrounded by oleanders, acacias and gums, a smaller cottage, various outhouses and the hangar. Craig made a faultless landing on the red airstrip and they descended and pushed the plane into the hangar where another Cessna was already housed.

They strolled over to the big house. Puffs of wind set vermilion dust-devils whirling across the bush. A tame kangaroo hopped to meet them.

'A young one whose mother was killed in a collision with one of our trucks. Her name is Hoppity and she's Sally's pet. Sally is our daughter aged five,' Craig explained to Dave. 'Our second daughter, Belinda, is four. You can't have an only child in the outback. It wouldn't be fair.'

Vera Craig, a smiling freckled young woman, met them at the door and they went into the house. The kitchen adjoined the living-room and was nearly as large. Vera laughed as Dave exclaimed at the size of the enormous refrigerator when he went with her to help her get the drinks.

'Wittenoom is over a hundred miles away and that's our nearest shopping centre.'

'Living in the outback must need careful housekeeping,' he observed. 'You can't go back for that odd packet of cigarettes you forgot.'

'One soon gets used to it. We fly in once a week. Really, it's easy.'

The little girls had been playing in the garden and now they trotted in to meet the newcomers and beg for cool drinks which they each sucked from the bottle through a straw.

Phil watched Dave's expression as he talked to the children, their wide-eyed faces and fair heads on a level with his own. They were friendly and obviously delighted at having visitors in the house. Hoppity was with them.

'Come and see Hoppity's bed,' said Sally. 'She sleeps in a sack.'

The sack hung from a peg on the wall of the verandah outside the kitchen and Hoppity leapt into it head first, leaving limbs sticking out at awkward angles. The children giggled happily. Suddenly there was turmoil in the sack and Hoppity's face reappeared with its large soft eyes and coy downturned eyelashes.

'Come out,' ordered Sally, and the young 'roo emerged and landed on the floor with a bump. 'Would you like to feel in her pouch?'

Dave obliged and was pleasantly surprised by its silky warmth.

'Lucky baby 'roos,' he said. 'Nice lining for the carry-cot.'

He was clearly at home with children and animals. Phil wondered if he missed his own. She was tempted to try to catch Dave out – to put a quick unexpected question that would trap him into revealing his true identity. But she desisted. The saturnine hardness of his face had melted and he looked young and almost happy. The other is the mask, she thought. This is the man. Or were they both the man? Of course. Everybody was many-sided. She was choosing what she liked best. But if you take a man you take all of him the good, the bad, the charm, the churlishness, the wonderful and the fearful. This man – she was more than ever certain that he was Franz's brother – intrigued her. She felt superior and yet a little ashamed that she should be able to guess so much about him while he believed himself unknown – like an eavesdropper or a Peeping Tom.

'I have a parrot – a green and yellow one,' announced Belinda. 'Don't you want to —'

'Children, it's time for lunch. Go and wash your hands,' called Vera. 'Run along now! You can show off your parrot later, Belinda.'

That afternoon Dave flew over the terrain with Mr Collins and Victor Craig while the two young women occupied themselves about the house and garden. It was a luxury to Vera to have a woman friend of her own generation to talk to.

'Though it's not nearly as lonely as it was,' she admitted. 'There's always some engineer or prospector flying in to see Vic these days, and, of course, we go to the coast quite often. Everything's livened up. Your friend's nice, isn't he? He's got what it takes – plus.'

'I've only met him twice. I know very little about him.'

Vera raised an eyebrow. 'Funny. I had the impression you'd known each other for ever.'

Phil wanted to say, 'I knew his brother very well.' Instead she answered, 'There are some people like that. You meet for the first time but you feel you've known them – as you say – for ever.'

It was an admission and Vera smiled. Phil's reputation was 'hard to get'. She said:

'Ah, well, I gather he may be coming to stay here in the cottage while he explores the area. It'll be nice to have him around. He can fly the second Cessna, I suppose?'

'Yes, he and —' Phil bit her lip and broke off. She had

begun to say 'He and his brother are both pilots.' So now it seemed that she, like Dave, must guard her tongue.

When the men came back in the evening Dave said:

'I'd like to stretch my legs – go for a walk.'

'Take him to the canyon, Phil,' said Vera. 'I know Vic still has a lot of problems to iron out with Mr Collins, and I'll be busy seeing to the kids and getting dinner. It's a nice stroll – not too far. Don't hurry. I'll feed Sally and Belinda first and we'll eat whenever we feel like it.'

'We'll go to the canyon in the car, and then climb down,' said Phil.

As they went out to the Holden Dave pointed to the barred steel fender above the front bumper.

'What's that?'

She laughed. 'Haven't you seen a kangaroo fender before? I s'pose not. But about this time of evening 'roos are at their most active. It's easy to hit one in the dusk or after dark. It suddenly springs onto the track and is dazzled by the lights. You could have a nasty accident.'

She drove the car fast and well across country, mowing down the spiky spinifex, following faint tracks between fantastic red anthills and mulga trees.

'I've seen anthills like these in Zambia, on the copper belt,' said Dave. 'They could be miniature mediaeval castles and towers.'

'Some are twenty feet high,' she said. 'Oh, look at that 'roo family party!'

She stopped the car and the bounding 'roos stopped too, the big male in the lead standing six foot tall.

'He's as tall as you,' she laughed.

'Shall I go and stand back to back with him?'

'He'd be off and away like a flash. Look. There's a joey peeping out of his mother's pouch. The mothers are so brave. If you hunted her down she'd run till it was hopeless and then she'd throw out the joey and draw off the pursuers herself.'

The little party of five animals of various sizes and ages bounded away into the bush and Dave and Phil watched them out of sight. Others came into view and Dave gazed at them in delight.

'Kangaroos in their own setting – my first.'

She stole a glance at his face, serene and amused, as he had looked when he was talking to the little girls, as if many cares had fallen away from him.

'The canyon is only a short way from here,' she said. 'We'll leave the car.'

He followed her down the narrow trail and suddenly there it was – a deep scarlet gash caused by centuries of erosion. Far down in its violet depths was a stream with trees, grass and flowers nourished by a long horizontal gush of water cascading into a clear pool from a rocky outcrop covered with fern and moss.

'Our spring,' she said, guiding him down the sloping wall. 'You should see the canyon after the rains, it's a real torrent then. You'll find this a bit of a scramble but if you follow me you'll be all right. I know the hand and footholds by heart.' At last they stood in the glade on the floor of the canyon. A silver ghost-gum rose tall and elegant, a masthead shimmering above acacias and willows and the pool of shining water.

'A lovely place for a picnic,' he said. 'A spring. More rewarding than some of the mineral deposits I saw today.'

He leaned against the rock, cupping his hands and drinking from the cold source of the water. He dashed it over his forehead and held his bare brown arms and wrists beneath it. 'Delicious!'

'Your watch!' she exclaimed.

'Waterproof.' He laughed, with a glance at his wrist. When he laughed his face was young and his eyes very gay, accentuating his likeness to Franz. Suddenly, seeing him like that, she caught her breath, the old dangerous magic stirring her blood and quickening her senses. She tried to calm her voice.

'Are you going to stay here in the outback, Dave?'

'Yes – it's good to be away from it all.'

'Away from what? What have you given up to come here?'

He took a step towards her and caught her arms. His hands were still cold from the spring water as they touched her bare flesh.

'Phil! I don't know what you guess – but can't you just accept me as I am? You must realize that I'm trying to make a new start. Isn't that enough for the present?'

'Can one simply slough off the old life, whatever and wherever it may be?'

'One can try. Must you make me dredge up the things I most desperately want to forget?'

She sat on the warm grass and he sat beside her. His face had darkened and his restless hands sought his cigarette case and lighter. She refused the cigarette he offered her.

'Why should you do this, Phil?'

'Do what?'

'Torture me with questions – with hints. You did it the first time we met. Why? I'm out of my normal context here.

Why can't I be allowed to stop and start again? There are times in life when people have to do that. Make new beginnings.'

She was silent as dusk seeped into the canyon, chilling them both. Birds flew down to the water and to their nests in the trees surrounding it. Have I the right to probe? she wondered, and was answered by her intense awareness of the man so close to her.

'Because I know – or rather guess – too much. Your brother wanted to marry me.'

'My brother?' His tone was sharp.

'Franz Morley. He told me about you, Dave – about Storm and how your family fought to keep her out. But she won . . . and now it's you who are out. There were children too – her daughter by her first husband and a baby boy by you.'

He crushed out his cigarette, making sure that the dry grass could not ignite. He was silent, his face drawn and hard. She knew now that she was right. At last he said:

'I suppose you guessed because we look alike and I was fool enough to keep my name in a sort of a way. Curious how one feels one's identity as a human being is threatened without one's own name.'

'Yes, your name – Dave – but mostly, of course, because of your resemblance to Franz. It's very strong, you know. Only your expression is different. In every way you are a darker version of your brother. Darker hair and skin —'

'Darker experiences, darker moods. All right, Phil. I give in. You know the truth. Please keep it to yourself. If I desert Storm for long enough she'll want her freedom. She says now that she'll never give me mine, but I know to the

contrary. It won't be long before there'll be another man –
there has to be for Storm – and then perhaps I can get myself off the hook.' He spoke bitterly.

'And the children?' asked Phil quietly.

'I'd only fight for their custody if I was sure she . . . might
be harmful to them. Otherwise it would be cruel to separate
them and Gaby isn't mine, though I love her as if she were.
Storm idolizes Garth. I find it impossible to believe she
might hurt them – and yet —'

'You fear she might?'

He rose to his feet and put out his hands to draw her up.

'Who can tell what another human being might do?
Storm is – unbalanced. Let's talk about you.'

'Why – about me?'

'I think I'm glad you've guessed. And now that you know
so much about me you must know too that I want to make
love to you.'

He pulled her into his arms and said against her hair. 'The
moment I saw you I wanted you – terribly.'

'Do you always get what you want?' she asked breath-
lessly.

'Sometimes I get what I deserve and that's not so good.'

He tipped up her face with a long determined finger. He
had Franz's hands but more audacious, more persistent.
Taught by Storm, she thought, by other women. She re-
belled at his power over her and struggled to free herself.

'Darling, don't be silly? We are two lonely people in a
very lonely place. What's a kiss between friends?'

'We aren't friends.' Her voice was low. She was rigid in
his embrace, determined not to yield.

'We could be.'

His lips were on hers. A kiss – only a kiss. It was a spring in the thirstland.

Nature's spring cascaded down the rock face into the pool with a cool song. Birds twittered and the night breeze rustled the sharp hard leaves of the gum. Near the car, on the canyon bank, three kangaroos grazed peacefully, the joey between his mother and her mate.

Phil's head whirled. Dave ... Franz ... Dave. She closed her eyes and Dave felt her resistance ebb. He held her close. She was everything Storm was not and he found himself moved by a tenderness Storm had never inspired in him. If only he were free – really free!

8

THE THREAT

THE LATE SPRING DAY WAS COLD AND SINCE HIS wife's death Hector Morley had felt the cold. A raw creeping chill had invaded his bones and settled deep inside him as if the absence of her physical presence and spiritual warmth had deprived him of a protective radiance and left him in a no man's land untouched by sun and light. He pulled his big easy chair closer to the fire and held out his hands to the blaze, old gnarled corded hands discoloured with brown liver-spots and graced by well kept nails.

Outside the study window a black south-easter flecked with rain tossed the branches and battered the early roses. He heard the dogs bark as a car parked under the palm and he knew that in a few moments he would have to face an awkward interview. How would Storm attack – with tears, or venom, or both.

He had only recently returned from the Transvaal after nearly a month with Franz at Golden Grass. He had been pleased to see his son's progress and methods. The lad was making a good thing of the farm and Hector had taken quite a fancy to the Malans over the rise and that nice yellow-haired child, Hortense Malherbe. She was obviously crazy about Franz, but, as far as Hector could judge, the young man was brotherly in his attitude towards her. And Hector reckoned he was quite a good judge. For instance, why was

that Australian girl's photograph still on Franz's desk? He
never talked about her. The thing was supposed to be over,
whatever it might have been, yet he couldn't bring himself
to put that picture away. Hector might be 'the Old Man' to
his family but he had not forgotten what it was to be young.
Though, since Marie was no longer with him, he tried not
to think about it – Marie as a bride, as a young mother, as
the homemaker, as his lover and companion. These days he
moved and talked automatically in a queer detached way as
if nothing that happened around him could really touch him
anymore. It was like the chill in his bone marrow, it was the
beginning of dying, the shadow of the Reaper cutting him
off from life, even, in a way, from his own family. He would
never have thought such a thing possible. The family was a
unit. If one member died, the others should be able to take
over and make good the loss in some way or another –
alleviate it, at all events. But Marie had been the heart of the
family. Without her the unit might fall apart. Was Dave's
defection the first symptom of disintegration? How close the
gap? Fight Storm, throw her out, and Dave would return.
He braced his shoulders as he heard the clip of her heels on
the polished floor of the hall leading into his study and he
turned his head to see her in the doorway.

'Storm,' he said. 'Come in and shut the door.'

She had not seen him since the funeral and she was shocked
at his appearance. His suit hung on his broad scrawny frame
and his eyes were sunken but his mouth under the grey
moustache was firm as a trap. He rose to meet her. They both
knew that this was not a social occasion nor a sympathetic
visit to welcome him back to his house of sorrow, and he saw
at once that she had come to accuse him. She was thinner

than she had been, her voluptuous features had hardened, she was tight lipped and her eyes were brilliant as agate.

'I don't have to tell you that Dave has left me – disappeared into the blue,' she said.

'I heard so.'

He motioned her to a chair and she sat down, not in her usual relaxed, almost abandoned way, but tense, her hands on the arms, her back straight. He too let himself down once more in the big leather armchair, sighing slightly. He was full of rheumatism this morning – change in the wind, no doubt.

'You heard so!' She laughed bitterly. 'Can't we talk frankly? You know where he is. You must know. That's what I've come to find out.'

'You won't find it out from me for the simple reason that I do not – repeat *not* – know where my son is. I'd be interested to hear what you can tell me about the whole affair.'

She took a letter from her bag and passed it over to him. 'He left this. Read it!'

He put on his spectacles and read it carefully. She watched him as a hunting beast watches its chosen quarry. This old man had always been her implacable foe. He had been formally polite for his wife's sake, and, for the same reason, he had offered her the hospitality of his home. He had unbent a little when her son had grown into a sturdy child stamped with the Morley looks and endowed with the Morley strength and vigour, but fundamentally he had resented and mistrusted her. She thought that his grizzled hair and moustache looked unkempt, like a dog with its coat starting. Sick.

Storm. This isn't an easy letter to write. It admits failure –

the total failure of our marriage. After what you told me on the evening of my mother's funeral I can never live with you again. I am going away and you won't be able to find me. Only my lawyer, Warren Keller, will know my address in due course. If you must get in touch with me at any time you may do so through him. But he has instructions to keep my whereabouts secret. When you want your freedom you can divorce me on grounds of desertion. I shall never return to you.

Dave.

Hector folded the letter and handed it back to her, his face expressionless.

'He's made the situation quite clear, hasn't he?'

'You put him up to it – to get me out of the Morley clan.'

He struck the desk suddenly with his clenched fist.

'Rubbish! Dave is a man, not a child. If I'd had any real authority over him he would never have married you. As it is, he's had to learn his lesson for himself.'

Her eyes blazed. 'When he married me you cut him out of your will. You have a fortune and you give your other children presents but you allowed Dave nothing—'

'You live well enough.'

'Oh, no, I don't – we didn't – stuck here in this one horse village. We ought to have been able to travel, go where we liked and do what we liked. Even my furs and diamonds I owe to Sidney Barralet —'

'You owe them to his creditors. You ruined him with your extravagance. You have big ideas, my girl, and I have no intention of gratifying them. You invested in my son for his father's money but you misjudged your market.'

'I loved Dave,' she said.

'You love money too.'

She shrugged. 'You wouldn't help him while we were together, but you've helped him now. You must have done. We're in debt all over the place. If he's gone any further than Sir Lowry's Pass and across the mountains someone has paid his fare. Who paid it and where to? You have the answers and I've come here to get them.'

'You won't get them from me. As to Dave's decision to leave you, would you care to tell me what it was you told him on the evening of his mother's funeral? I too have questions that require answers.'

'We quarrelled. It was just another quarrel. He was upset and emotional that day, as you can imagine. I have a violent temper, I admit, and I lost it. But nothing was really changed between us —'

'Wasn't it?' he put in sharply. 'Your husband walks out on you and you say nothing was really changed.'

'No!' She spoke loudly and with heat. 'He didn't discover anything about me that he didn't already know – or guess. He had no real reason to walk out on me.'

'Whatever illusions you destroyed that day you cooked your goose, Storm. He'll never come back to you. You'd better make up your mind to that and divorce him for desertion as he suggests. It's easy in this country, and quick.'

'What's it worth to you to force my hand?'

'So you've come to bargain?' He rose as if in dismissal. 'You'd better go and see Dave's lawyer in that case. I don't do dirty work myself.'

'Nor do I,' she said. 'Be careful, Mr Morley!'

She sprang to her feet, and, for a moment, he thought that

she would reach up and claw at his eyes. He stared down at her contemptuously.

'If I divorce Dave he loses Garth,' she snapped.

'We'll see about that.'

'You're very high and mighty,' she said through clenched teeth. 'You wait, Hector Morley! I'll bring you low.'

'You've done that already. You've brought all of us low.'

'You've a lot to learn about me,' she said grimly.

'I can guess your capacity for wickedness. I should say it's unlimited.'

'All the more reason to watch your step, you arrogant interfering old man. Watch your step or I'll have my revenge.'

'You're wasting your histrionics, Storm. There's no audience to this play. Revenge is a grandiose term. It has a certain magnificence. There was a battleship called Revenge. Your threats aren't worthy of such a word. You don't revenge yourself on people because they refuse to bargain with you about money, even if you are avaricious and —'

He broke off as he felt the force of her knuckles strike him across the mouth, breaking his lip with something hard and sharp. A trickle of blood ran down his chin but his head was higher than ever. He glared at her down the high bridge of his nose. She was panting as if the blow had done nothing to ease her pent up fury. She put her hand to her throat and gulped. He could see the pulse beating in her neck as she fought to control herself.

'I shouldn't have done that,' she said at last. 'Please wipe your chin, there's blood on it.'

'And on your hand.' He offered her his handkerchief with a sardonic smile.

She lowered her hand with the cabuchon cat's eye ring on the middle finger and saw the stained knuckle. His blood not hers. She rubbed it off and returned his handkerchief.

'You've wrecked my marriage,' she said defensively. 'You've made it possible for Dave to leave me. You've encouraged him. I know it. I have my reasons for hating you.'

'Shall we try to be civilized – for Marie's sake? Shall we maintain the façade of tolerance? If you're in financial difficulties put the whole matter to Warren Keller and he can speak to me.'

'I'll do as you say,' she said. 'But I warn you I won't give Dave up. If I wait he'll come back to me. I have a certain power over him. He always comes back.'

'So he's left you before?'

'He's tried to – but he comes home exhausted, home to me. Crawling home like a dog.'

'A dog to its vomit,' he said icily.

She threw him a look of sheer malevolence before she snapped her handbag open and fumbled for her cigarette case with shaking fingers. The Old Man was ready with a light. His manners towards her had always been coldly impeccable. As he struck the match he saw the furrow between her quivering eyebrows. Her control was almost at its limit.

'Was there anything else?' he asked.

She inhaled deeply and blew the smoke out of her nostrils.

'Very much so. We don't live in a vacuum, you know. People talk about Dave and me, always have done. They talk about you. What the hell are we going to tell them when they ask where Dave is?'

'What have you been telling them?'

'I said he'd gone prospecting in the Transvaal in the area of Golden Grass – that you'd be seeing him.'

'A good enough story.'

She moved her shoulders impatiently. 'That story may hold water for a couple of weeks, but as months go by – if they do – it's going to wear pretty thin.'

'Then tell them the truth. Say he's left you and you intend to divorce him.'

'Stop putting the heat on me! I won't divorce him. You're saddled with me – the lot of you – and you'd better accept that fact.'

He made a gesture of indifference.

'What will *you* say?' she persisted. 'When people ask *you* about Dave?'

'I'll tell them the truth – part of it. I'll say I've no idea where he is. That he must have heard of mineral desposits somewhere and he's probably investigating. Could be anywhere. He's secretive. I'd advise you to do the same if the whole truth is so distasteful to you.'

'The family – the precious family – had better stick to the same story,' she spat at him.

'I agree.'

'The children ask,' she said. 'They miss him. Garth is too young to suffer but Gaby does. She cries at night.'

'Poor little Gaby. Send her to me as usual. I'll give her a picture of a prospector's life – a sort of western. I'll invest this disappearance with false glamour.'

'It's not knowing – not knowing anything! I hate him for that and I blame you. You're responsible, say what you like. You're behind it. Dave would never have done this dirty trick without your backing.'

Hate contorted her face and he saw with sharp satisfaction that he had humiliated her as she had humiliated him by marrying his son before her husband was cold in his grave. His worn proud face was more expressive than he knew.

'I'll never forgive you,' she said. 'One day I'll make you pay. Not only in money either.'

She was a tall woman but he towered over her.

'I don't like threats. Go home now and send your children here this afternoon. I'll talk to Gaby.'

When she had gone he sat down with his head in his hands. He did not underrate his adversary. Storm was indeed capable of revenge – of doing him harm. Dave had warned him. What a fool Dave had been and what a price he was paying for his folly! Could a man live with evil and preserve his own soul? Could the innocence of children survive the proximity of so much venom and violence? Would she ever strike them as she had struck him? Were they safe with her? He shuddered, a prey once again to the creeping cold that seemed to penetrate his whole being. What had Marie so persistently said? 'Overcome evil with good'. After his fashion he had tried. He felt very tired and rather sick.

Storm stood in the windy rain-spattered sunshine and opened the door of her car. Amber leaned against her, warm and heavy. She would like to have kicked out at the labrador but he might have retaliated with a nip. She got into the car and slammed the door and a few seconds later she was driving down the avenue of tall gums laden with their abundance of bright flowers. Her burst of rage had cooled and she was not totally displeased. She had learned nothing

from the Old Man but he had implied that he would grant
her an allowance if he considered it necessary. She reckoned
she could put up a case. He had really been rather forbearing
when she had lost her temper. Or had he merely treated her
as a creature beneath contempt? She saw again the bloodied
curling lip, the disdainful eyes, cold and steely. How she
loathed those proud gimlet eyes that expressed more than
words! She felt her throat and cheeks burn. He could make
her feel as if he saw right through her. Now she came to
think of it, he had never once denied in so many words that
he had helped or advised Dave to leave her, on the other
hand he had stated baldly that he had no knowledge of his
son's whereabouts. By and large, he had discovered more
from her in the interview than she from him. He was shrewd
and cunning, he meant to prise her out of the family and she
abominated him.

On her return from Blue Horizon Storm went through
her house onto the terrace. She found the Malay workman
busy laying the paving in the walled patio she and Dave had
designed. A fountain played in the middle of a miniature
rose garden and a pergola of climbing roses and cup-of-gold
covered the partially completed terrace outside the French
doors. It would be charming to sit out here on summer
evenings, but with Dave gone what was the use? She tossed
her head. He'd come back. He wouldn't be able to stay away
from her. She'd write to him through that damn lawyer and
ask him – even implore him – to come back. He'd never be
able to resist her.

The workman rose from his haunches and tipped his cap
as she came out and stood staring down at him. He observed

that there was an odd expression on her face as if she was looking past him at someone else – *'n spook.* Suddenly she smiled
and he realized that the ghost had disappeared. She was seeing
him, Ali.

'You're making a good job of it, Ali.'

His calm Oriental features relaxed and brightened at her
praise.

'It's sommer tricky fitting the slates together.'

He glanced down at the complicated mosaic of the different
shaped paving slates – thin and softly coloured like the blue-
grey plumage of the ring-doves cooing and flirting in the
little garden.

'I see you're putting cement in the cracks already. Why
don't you lay them all first?'

He spread his slender craftsman's hands with a slight
grin.

'Because Madam's children come to pick them up and
play with them.'

She frowned. 'That's naughty of them. Phoebe should
watch them better than to let them do that.'

'It's all right. Not much harm done.'

'The cement overflows onto the slate,' she remarked. 'How
do you clean it?'

'I have some acid for that. I give it a good clean up last
thing. After that the job is finished and klaar.'

He was rather a shabby little man with the sleek black hair
and deft hands of the Cape Malay. His intelligent almond
eyes were alive with humour and kindliness. No wonder the
children hung about him – and Phoebe too, for that matter.

'You mustn't let the children be a nuisance,' she said.
'Especially Garth. He's only a toddler and very mischievous.'

'I like children. The little girl was spraying the roses yesterday with her plastic water pistol. There was only water in it but I told the gardener to be careful or she'd try to fill it with real insecticide from his can.'

'Where on earth did she get a water pistol from?'

He chuckled. 'One of the little boys at her school.'

Storm laughed, her temper almost restored. 'They start young these days! Tell Phoebe to give you some tea and cake if you want it. She's in the yard hanging up the washing.'

'I won't take nothing, dankie, Madam. I have my food with me.'

She nodded, remembering that the Malays were never any bother about meals. They ate only what they brought with them. When a coloured girl married a Malay it was always hurtful to her mother that she no longer accepted the delicacies of her parents' home. She ate and thought and prayed as a Moslem, she bore her babies in the Malay tradition with a flower opening at her bedside and she was buried facing Mecca in the Malay cemetery.

Storm left Ali to his work and went into the house. Garth would be awake now, she'd go and play with him. In half an hour Phoebe would wheel him in his push-cart to fetch Gaby from her nursery school. Already they had begun to adapt themselves to a fatherless home. At first they had kept asking for Dave – even Garth, who at fourteen months old was surprisingly articulate – but now, after over a month without him, the little boy was beginning to forget his father. It was Gaby who remembered and missed him, but finding her constant questions irritated her mother she took them to her aunt Magda instead.

'Has Daddy gone far away like Granny?' she had asked Magda. 'Will he never come back?'

'One day he'll come back, Gaby,' Magda had replied.

'Where is he? Mommy won't tell me.'

'He's gone to work in another country. When he's finished his work he'll come back.'

'When, Aunt Magda?'

'Nobody knows, darling. One day.' With that the little girl had had to be content.

In the following weeks Gaby often saw her aunt and her grand-father at Blue Horizon. She loved to wheel Magda's baby, Hector, in his pram.

'He's lovely, isn't he?' she'd say, stroking his silky fair hair. 'And good, much gooder than Garth.'

'Yes, he's lovely,' Magda would agree gravely. 'He's like his Daddy. But when he's walking and running about like Garth he'll be full of nonsense.'

Ali, the Malay, broke his arm that October and the paving job had to wait till the middle of December to be continued. On Christmas Eve he was still busy cleaning up the overflow cement with special acid. Once Gaby wanted to fill her water pistol from the jar and Ali stopped her just in time. After which he said to Storm, who had come out to pick roses:

'Madam mus' please tell Miss Gaby she mus' *never* touch this stuff. It's not water. It burns. I keep the lid on when I'm not using it, but it's dangerous. Tonight I put it in the tool shed but tomorrow I am using it again.'

He was conscious of Madam's eyes staring at him but not really focusing properly – as if she saw that *spook* over his shoulder again. He had noticed her looking like that once before – the day the little girl had wanted to fill her pistol with the gardener's insecticide. Somehow the look had formed a haunting picture in his mind. It had given him the shivers then and it did so now. She seemed to return slowly from some far off place and now she really saw Ali, but her eyes concealed some thought he did not understand.

'Tomorrow is Christmas Day, Ali. Had you forgotten?'

'I'm a Malay,' he replied with dignity. 'I keep Moslem holidays. I can finish the job on Christmas Day as well as any other.'

'We'll all be out.'

'I'll come in the afternoon. I only have to clean up. It's better if the children are out.' He smiled. 'They want to help and that's dangerous when I'm working with this stuff.'

As if his words had reminded her of something important she called imperiously to Gaby. 'Come here at once, Gaby!'

The child approached hesitantly from the rose-bed.

'I didn't do it,' she said quickly, anticipating a rebuke. 'Ali told me not to touch his stuff, so I filled my pistol from the fountain!' She turned the little red plastic pistol in her hand and sent a jet of water into the heart of a rose.

'You aim well,' said Storm, 'but I'll keep this little pistol for you, Gaby, until you're sensible enough to know that you must never fill it with anything except water. First you wanted to fill it with insecticide and next with acid! It's safer with me.'

She took the toy from the child. Gaby's eyes brimmed and her lower lip trembled.

'Don't snivel,' said Storm. She took aim and sent a spray of water full into the small distressed face. 'That'll wash your tears away!'

Gaby gasped and began to cry in earnest.

'I'm playing with you,' said her mother. 'Here comes Garth. Your turn now. Wash his face and aim straight. The face is the target.'

Gaby gulped and took the pistol back from her mother. As Garth and Phoebe came onto the terrace she swung round and released its contents into her little brother's face, but the toy was almost empty and all he received was a cold trickle. His mother laughed as he chased Gaby on his sturdy toddler's legs and cried out, 'Mine! Mine!'

'It's his turn,' said Storm, and she recharged the pistol at the fountain and gave it to Garth. His fat chubby hands squeezed the trigger and sent a spray of water into Phoebe's face. It spilled over her collar.

'Don't do that!' she exclaimed in irritation.

But her mistress mocked at her. 'A wash won't hurt your face or your collar. This is a game. Garth was only joking. Now, Garth, another shot for Gaby as it's her pistol and then it must be given back to me. I'll take care of it. Tomorrow, on Christmas Day, if Gaby's a good girl, she can have it back and we can all play again. Cowboys and Indians maybe, or just plain "wash your face".'

Ali stood watching them without amusement, his mild gaze on the little girl who would be deprived of her toy through his fault. She'd done no harm. She hadn't even made as much mess as her mother was doing. He shook his head. Phoebe was looking sulky, Gaby had cheered up and Garth and his mother were gaily excited. Mrs Morley was slipping the toy pistol into her bag. The movement seemed to Ali sinister. It was always that way. The white people shot each other, natives hit each other over the head with sticks and the coloured people carried knives. He had a knife in his own pocket. There was no harm in carrying a knife if you didn't drink or smoke dagga. Ali did neither. Too many of his people betrayed their religion these days. They had learned to drink from the coloured people and deliberately forgot that a good Malay never touches alcohol. Somehow, seeing the little red plastic pistol drop into Mrs Morley's bag had affected him as unpleasantly as it did to see a drunk lad draw a knife and threaten a friend.

Ali had gone and the children were already in bed when Franz drove over from Blue Horizon to see his sister-in-law. She was sitting outside in the almost completed patio, and, as he joined her, he thought that she looked both beautiful and very lonely. She was not the sort of woman who ought to be spending Christmas Eve by herself. She jumped up to greet him, surprise and pleasure reflected in her eyes and in the gesture of her outstretched hands.

'Franz! How nice! When did you arrive?'

'Yesterday. So did Kev and Colleen and the children. I came over to check that you and Gaby and Garth are coming to Blue Horizon for Christmas mid-day dinner tomorrow. And I've brought a few things for the kids' Christmas stockings.'

'So we're still part of the family? Yes, we were counting on being included at the family Christmas reunion. What will you drink? Whisky —'

'Beer, please. Can I see Garth and Gaby?'

'They may be asleep already. But we'll go straight up to the nursery and we can have our drinks afterwards.'

She took him upstairs. The nursery curtains were drawn,

dimming the evening light. The shadowy room was filled
with peace and the sleepiness of children who had been in the
sun and air all afternoon. Gaby sat up and rubbed her eyes
as Storm and Franz entered. Suddenly the child uttered a
loud joyous cry and flung out her arms.

'Daddy! Daddy's come back!'

Storm turned on the light. Garth emerged from the
stupefying borderline of slumber and opened his large black
eyes. Gaby turned away and buried her face in the pillow.

'It's your Uncle Franz,' said Storm. 'He's come to stay
with Grandpa for Christmas, like your Uncle Kevin and
Aunt Colleen and Huddie and Pam.'

Garth chortled a welcome but Gaby was weeping quietly
and unchildishly and refused to turn her head.

'Oh, leave her,' said Storm impatiently. 'She's being a
silly little drip again.'

Franz hugged his nephew and then he went and sat on
the edge of the little girl's bed. He asked Storm to leave them
alone and she kissed the back of Gaby's head perfunctorily
and hugged Garth.

'Good-night, children. Don't keep your uncle. You'll find
me – and your beer – on the patio, Franz.'

He looked after her as she left the room. She was wearing
a sort of pyjama suit with a filmy transparent top that showed
her bra and the bare flesh between it and her matching hipster
slacks. She hadn't been expecting him, Franz thought, but
she was seductively dressed. He put his arms gently round
Gaby and turned her so that her small wet face was close to
his own.

'Your Daddy will come home,' he promised. 'He's away
doing a job and has to finish it. Next year he'll be home.'

'When is next year, Uncle Franz?'

'Soon. Tomorrow I'll show you on the calendar – when you come to Blue Horizon for Christmas dinner. We'll have fun tomorrow. Your cousins from up-country will be there. Hudson is your special friend, isn't he?'

Her tears had dried on her cheeks and now her smile broke.

'I have another friend. Johnny Clarke. He gave me my water pistol.'

'Show it to me, Gaby.'

'Mummy took it away from me but she's going to give it back tomorrow.'

'Well, bring it with you and we can play games.'

She laughed mischievously. 'I'll shoot you with it! I'll wash your face!'

'Will you, you monkey? We'll see about that. Now go to sleep. Happy dreams.'

She flung her arms round his neck and hugged him.

'Good-night, Uncle Franz.'

When he had tucked her in and patted the sleepy Garth he went out onto the patio.

'Gaby's looking forward to tomorrow,' he said.

Storm smiled. 'Every child loves Christmas. And Gaby is very fond of your father. I've never tried to influence her against him.' She was pouring his beer. Foam swelled above the rim of the tankard but she carried it steadily across to him without spilling a drop. He took it from her.

'Why should you?'

He saw her face change and darken. The sensual mouth thinned to a razor-sharp line, her eyes were molten with some pent up emotion that burned and consumed her.

'Because I hate your father more than anyone in the world. He's done everything in his power to ruin my life. He tried to stop Dave marrying me, and, when he failed in that, he turned Dave into a sort of pariah – cutting him out of his will, giving presents to you others but never to Dave, making it clear that not one cent of Morley money would ever come my way! Finally he encouraged Dave to desert me, made it possible for him. I know that! Warren Keller practically admitted as much. Your father's come between husband and wife in order to force me out of the beloved – the sacrosanct – family circle. I'll get even with him. You wait!'

She was panting – there was spittle on her compressed lips. Franz realized that she was hardly conscious of the fury of her own outburst. It had been spewed out of some sultry geyser of poison deep inside her. She's as mad as a rabid dog on this one subject, he thought, shocked and appalled. He sprang to his feet, his eyes, so like Dave's, blazing back at her.

'You're talking of my father – threatening him. You must be crazy to let yourself go like this – to me, his son!'

She blinked as if his reaction had brought her to her senses and she sank her convulsed face slowly into her hands. When she looked up again she was pale but controlled.

'I'm sorry,' she said in a low broken voice. 'Sometimes I think all this – Dave going off, disappearing God knows where – has driven me off my rocker. I can't help blaming your father. But I shouldn't have talked to you the way I did. Please forget it.'

The garden was almost in darkness, the white standard roses glimmering. Inside the house Storm's tape recorder was playing soft background music. Sentimental, soothing.

But Franz felt sick with the brief illuminating glimpse of the sort of thing his brother had probably had to contend with whenever she was in the mood. Her hatred of his father was obsessional – but not without reason, he had to admit. Suddenly Franz found that he was shivering in the warm midsummer evening as if the wings of some unknown evil had brushed across his skin. Upstairs the children slept, dreaming no doubt of Christmas stockings and the tree gay with coloured lights, glittering with tinsel and baubees. This was the season of peace and goodwill and their father was far away – the Lord and Warren Keller alone knew where. Storm came close to him.

'Please let's be friends, Franz. I'm lonely and unutterably sad. Sometimes even worse than that. Distraught, helpless to get my husband back. I love Dave. I want him. Can't you understand? People pity me and wonder. God knows what they're saying. It's not a nice situation for me or for the children.'

She was speaking calmly now, pleading for the understanding no member of his family would ever be likely to give her. Except, perhaps, Jules, who studied the minds and emotions of human beings as searchingly as he did their bodies. To Jules the physical and psychological were always complementary, never to be separated.

Her scent was in Franz's nostrils, aphrodisiac and penetrating and, angry as he was with her, he could not help realizing the extent of her frustration. In spite of her defiant belligerent front she was a woman abandoned and very much alone.

'You can make an end of it,' he said. 'Divorce Dave and be done with the lot of us.'

'There are the children,' she said. 'And I happen to want your brother back. Why should the Old Man take him from me?' She touched his arm. 'It's Christmas Eve – not a pleasant time to be alone. Stay and have supper with me.'

For some reason he thought suddenly of Phil and Pamamaroo and the day he had asked her to marry him. He too was sick with an inner loneliness. But he said, gently enough:

'I'm sorry. They're expecting me at home – at Blue Horizon. I must go back.'

'I'm sorry too,' she said. 'Go back to them then.'

'We'll see you and the children tomorrow.'

'Oh, yes, you'll see us tomorrow. I wouldn't miss tomorrow at Blue Horizon – not for worlds.'

She was standing between the French doors, an alluring silhouette. A sprig of mistletoe hung over her head. The room behind her was illuminated only by the pretty electric bulbs threading the branches of the Christmas tree in the corner. She saw his eyes on the mistletoe and laughed.

'Well?' she challenged him. 'It's the season's convention. Mistletoe.'

He put his hands lightly on her shoulders and brushed her upturned face with his lips. But suddenly her arms were round his neck and her mouth was pressed to his, soft and demanding. Her body was against his and he heard her whisper, 'You're lonely too, Franz. Stay!'

He disengaged himself, angry, tempted and disturbed. She let him go.

'So I'm the enemy – even to you. Very well, then Franz. So be it.'

She watched him go with the rangy stride so like his brother's. She turned back into the empty room with its Christmas trappings and its gay little tree. They were all against her, the whole close knit clan. But tomorrow she'd be in the fold – one of them for a day. Tomorrow.

9

LEOPARD IN THE FOLD

ON CHRISTMAS EVE DAVE HAD FLOWN DOWN TO Perth from the hot inland. True, the heat was dry, but never had he encountered such temperatures. Day after day it had soared past the century and the housewives, in their air-conditioned kitchens, had prepared food for their families with the somnolent lethargy of mid-summer in a territory backed by pitiless deserts that still held their secrets.

It was hot in Perth too, but the regular afternoon breeze cooled the air already freshened by the sea, and the Christmas night barbecue under the trees in the Collins' garden was held under near perfect conditions. Mrs Collins had completely recovered from her illness and Phil had almost decided that, after all, she would return to her job at Broken Hill after the holidays. Mrs Conway had written to tell her that she was greatly missed and needed. It was difficult to resist her appeal.

The guests had finished their sausages, steaks and potatoes-in-jackets all smoky and delicious from the grill, followed by ice cream and fruit, and a number of young couples had left the garden to dance on the terrace. Mr Collins was going round filling glasses with champagne. Dave and Phil sat on cushions on the grass at a little distance from the embers that still glowed in the open brick barbecue oven. Above them spread the pale branches of a fig tree laden with unripened fruit. In a few weeks the magpies would have a feast. Dave congratulated himself on having isolated Phil from the rest of the party for a few minutes. She wore yellow culottes and a satin blouse with full bishop sleeves and the men were in slacks and T-shirts, the sort of Christmas party they might have had in South Africa. But here there was the wide bend of the lovely Swan River and the lights of the yacht club up on the wooded bluff.

'Why?' Dave said urgently. 'Why should you go back to Broken Hill – so far away? Here at least I see you most weekends. If you go up there to New South Wales you'll be right out of my reach.'

'Perhaps that's how I want it.'

'You want to be nearer Ian Gray. It's so easy for him to get there from Adelaide.'

She smiled teasingly. 'Think what you like.'

'In that case I think you don't really love Ian Gray – or even Franz. You love me. I know it every time I touch you or look at you. I believe you know it too, Phil, though you won't admit it.'

'I don't know what I feel about you, Dave. It's all a turmoil. I have to get away and find out. When you're here I want you. When you aren't everything else comes into proportion. It's different – like being released from a spell.'

'Don't you think about me when I'm away?'

'I think about you,' she said honestly. 'But I see you more clearly.'

'My God, that sounds like the school marm talking! Tell me, then. Give me the works, don't spare me! How do you see me in those moments of perfect clarity?'

In the darkness, lit only by starlight and the glowing wood ash and very faintly from the lights up on the terrace of the house, her downcast profile was pure and classic, short dark hair falling forwards across the wide brow, thick lashes hiding her eyes. She spoke in a low voice.

'You've asked for it, Dave. I'll give it to you as fairly as I can. When you're away from me I see you dodging your responsibilities – leaving those little children to the care of a woman you know to be bad. Your family can't step in and take them from her. I don't know that I like it – the thing you've done.'

He stiffened. 'Running away?'

'That's how it seems to me.'

She saw his face change and become persuasive, and she thought, Now be careful, Phil. Watch out! He said:

'I could make a new life here with you. We could get custody of the children – bring them to Australia —'

'You aren't a free man, Dave. You're talking as if you were.'

'I mean to be. I will be. If you married me you could stay in your own country. I love Australia – even the heat and the hell of the inland. It's a wildly exciting country and there's gambling in my blood. I love all the new things that are happening in the north-west – your father's territory. I like working for him. And I think he likes and trusts me.'

'He trusts your work but he doesn't know your personal history.'

'He's a blunt man and he takes me as I am. Your mother asks feminine questions in her dreamy yet practical way – difficult ones to answer too. But, so far, I've dodged spilling the beans. Your father simply accepts me as a useful and reliable employee. He doesn't seem to guess about us. I think he believes you'll marry Gray one of these days.'

'He may be right. In any case, if my father knew you better – really knew you – he wouldn't approve of the mess you've left behind.'

Suddenly he was hurt and angry. She had never thrown his past mistakes at him to make him feel a heel. She'd seemed to respect the way he'd tackled his job in the heat and solitude of the iron ore country. He'd had every reason to believe that she found him more than a little attractive, and now, when he wanted to plan a real future with her as his wife, she turned against him.

'This is the country of new beginnings,' he said. 'Can't a man be allowed to forget his past?'

'Not while it's still his present as well. You don't know what the repercussions of your desertion may be – on the children, on your family, on you. What's the good of making plans when nothing has really been resolved between you and your wife?'

'Christmas and the New Year – it's the season for making plans and resolutions. Are you perfectly content to let everything ride? Don't you want a goal and a future as a woman, not a teacher? Don't you want someone to share all your hopes and dreams?'

'I don't know what I want.'

Her face grew solemn as she realized the truth of her words. After all, what right had she to criticize Dave? He was doing his best to make a new successful start – and what was she doing? Hiding away from all the vital issues. Once, if she had had the courage – and the love – she too might have been prepared to start afresh in a new country. But she had been afraid of severing her roots and deserting her parents. Desertion and a new beginning. Was it perhaps the better pattern in Dave's case? Might it have been in hers? Was she a greater coward than the harrassed young man she was presuming to judge?

The Mersey beat came to them across the garden – an old record, pulsing and compulsive with its offbeat rhythm.

'What'll they be doing now in South Africa?' she asked. 'Your folk . . . Franz . . .'

'At this minute?'

'Yes.'

He glanced at his watch. 'It's nine o'clock here, it'll be somewhere round three in the afternoon there. They'll be finishing a huge Christmas mid-day feast. It has to be mid-day because of the children – Kevin and Colleen's little Hudson and Pam, and our Gaby and Garth. But Pam and Garth and Magda's little Hector will probably be resting upstairs, so that'll leave only Huddie and Gaby to wear paper caps and blow tin whistles; and for their sakes the grown-ups will pretend to be gay while all the time they'll be haunted by my mother's ghost. Christmas was *her* day.'

'The grown-ups? Your father, Kevin and Colleen, Magda and Jules and Franz. You see, I know them all. Will Storm be there?'

'Yes,' he said. 'Because my mother would have wished it, because she's still a Morley and because my father would never allow the children to become estranged from the family. By now Gaby will be getting tired and over excited, naughty perhaps . . .'

He broke off and drew Phil to her feet and led her into the deeper shadows of the fig tree.

'Please, Phil, don't make me think of Blue Horizon now.'

'No,' she whispered. 'Your mother won't be the only ghost at that family gathering. There'll be you – all of them wondering where you are – who you're with. Even Franz never guessing . . .'

A bat flew past them and she uttered a little cry and ducked her head against his chest. His arms encircled her, crossing behind the small of her back, drawing her to him in the movement familiar to them both. His bent head sought her lifted face and his lips nuzzled her ears and sent the blood tingling through her veins. His mouth was soft and tender. She knew the firm texture of his skin, the smoky smell of it that held no reminder of Franz. Only one thing could assuage the hunger in them both and her head was beginning to spin. She pushed him from her.

'Let's go and dance. People will be wondering where I am. This is my party tonight.'

He followed her reluctantly up to the terrace.

While the stars shone in Western Australia the sun was still high in the Cape Peninsula. The day outside was hot and breathless but it was reasonably cool in the big dining-room at Blue Horizon. The remains of the Christmas pudding had been removed and Elijah had passed round the coffee and left the silver coffee tray in front of Magda in case anyone wanted a second cup. In other years the percolator would have been set before the hostess, but that ritual had gone with so much else since the mistress of Blue Horizon was no longer there.

Franz thought that Colleen had made the table look gay and pretty with the big silver bowl of Peace roses, the many-coloured crackers and the little silver lattice baskets of bonbons and dried fruit, and somehow they had got through the meal with a show of good will and appreciation. The Old Man had arranged the seating plan himself. He had put Colleen on his right and Magda on his left. Next to Magda came Kevin, then Storm with Jules at the end of the table opposite him. Little Hudson on Jules' left, then Gaby with Franz between her and Colleen.

Franz found his small companion in a highly excitable state and Huddie was not much better. The little boy's unruly black curls had been smarmed down by Colleen, but his big vivacious dark eyes were full of mischief and he was showing off and teasing Gaby, who was at her most feminine, dimpling at him and bossing him by turns.

'Watch them, Franz,' said Jules, amused. 'The man asserts himself and the woman bewitches him and pushes him around till he's totally bewildered and she has him just where she wants him. The feminine instinct displays itself at an early age.'

'You're right,' laughed Storm. 'Milady is wearing a new dress and she's very pleased with herself. It's the height of fashion. I found her at my dressing table this morning trying out my lipsticks.'

'All for Huddie – lucky Huddie,' grinned Franz. But he was thinking that the children contributed more than they knew to the missing Christmas spirit. So did old Lettie whose turkey had been done to a turn and whose Christmas pudding had arrived in an aura of flame.

Franz had a curious feeling of being a spectator at a Christmas play. Not one of them – except the two children – had the heart for this gathering. Hector was playing the part of the host with benevolent dignity but his face was ravaged.

Magda was clearly trying to remember her mother's maxim
'overcome evil with good': Colleen was using all her Irish
charm to make the party go while Kevin, who was a man
of great silences, was doing his utmost to respond to his
sister-in-law's chatter. For, to do her justice, Storm had
evidently decided to bury all feuds for the time being and
her attitude towards this family in which she was regarded
as an interloper was gay and slightly teasing towards Kevin
and Jules on either side of her. Every now and again she drew
Franz into the conversation across the table and he had to
admit than she was a superb actress. No trace of her profound
abiding resentment of her father-in-law was visible in her
behaviour and her spectacular good looks were never more
vivid than on this summer's day. She seemed to glow with
the festive spirit that eluded the others and her long oblique
eyes were brilliant with hidden amusement and even triumph.
Why triumph? Perhaps because she was here at all – still
accepted, the intruder who refused to be ousted. Upstairs,
her Morley son, Garth, was asleep in the temporary nursery
with Colleen's little Pam and Magda's baby Hector. Beside
Franz Storm's little daughter flirted with her cousin Hudson,
flashing small white teeth, tossing her curls and bursting
into laughter as she and Huddie tugged at a cracker with all
their might and Huddie nearly fell over backwards as it came
apart with a small satisfying explosion. Franz, who was in
charge of the champagne, had refilled Storm's glass several
times and once she had looked up at him and smiled pro-
vocatively as she held out her glass.

'Thanks for the Dutch courage.'

'Do you need it?'

'In this house, yes.'

As he resumed his seat Storm said: 'Tell us about Australia. What will your girl friend be doing today?'

'I haven't a girl friend in Australia. I had when I was there but when we said goodbye that was it. However, I guess it'll be much the same in Perth as it is here – a mid-summer Christmas. Could be a day on the river, a picnic —'

'It'll be night time now,' said Jules. 'They're several hours ahead of us, aren't they?'

'Yes, six or seven, something like that.'

'Let's pull some more crackers!' Gaby tugged at Franz's sleeve. 'Mummy promised that after the crackers were all finished she'd give me back my water pistol.'

'And then what will you do?'

'I'll play cowboys and Indians. I'll play with Gran'pa.'

'You'd better play with Huddie.'

She pursed up her lips and looked mysterious.

So the last of the crackers were pulled and the children donned their paper crowns and collected their trinkets in little heaps with the tiny silver charms the Christmas pudding had yielded – a slipper, a bell, a wishbone, a horseshoe.

'D'you think we can get down now?' Gaby asked Franz as Magda helped herself and her father to more coffee. Jules was offering liqueurs, the rich brown of Van der Hum, the ruby of Cherry Brandy, the emerald of Crème de Menthe. Their reflections sparkled in the silver tray before him.

'Ask your Grandfather,' said Franz. 'I'm sure he'll let you and Huddie get down now. Then you can play cowboys and Indians to your hearts' content outside.'

'Gran'pa, may we go, please?' asked Gaby.

Old Hector smiled at the child, benevolent and kindly despite the sense of loss that weighed on him this day as never before, haunted as he was by the shades of his wife and of his absent son, Dave. Storm he treated with customary frigid politeness.

'Yes, you may get down, Gaby – you and Huddie. But first you must say grace.'

The children bent their heads and the grown-ups did likewise as Gaby and Huddie gabbled in unison. 'For what we have received may the good Lord make us truly grateful. Amen.'

As the word 'Amen' echoed round the table Huddie and Gaby scrambled down from their chairs and Gaby ran to her mother.

'My water pistol, Mommy. You said I could have it.'

'You can.'

Storm drew the red plastic toy from her bag and gave it to the child. 'You can have a sip of my champagne too.'

Gaby laughed and gulped down half a glass of the fizzy golden wine. She was elated, beside herself with merriment.

'Can I really shoot Gran'pa just for fun, like you told me to?' she whispered in her mother's ear.

Storm smiled. 'Of course. He won't mind on Christmas Day. Anyhow, I dare you to.'

The Old Man looked at Gaby benignly from his patriarchal seat at the head of the table. She was flourishing her little pistol rather wildly.

'What game is this? Are we in the Wild West?'

'Yes, yes,' she cried. 'Cowboys and Indians. I'm a cowboy!'

She ran round the table past Jules, waving the pistol, her

little gold paper crown slipping back from her curls, hazel eyes dancing.

'Hy!' said Jules. 'Where are you off to?' And suddenly Franz remembered what she had said the night before and realized her intention. The Old Man would most certainly not be amused to receive a jet of cold water in the face. As she scampered past his chair he turned and snatched at her frilly skirt, pulling her up short.

'What's the idea, my little one?'

She whirled round. 'I'm a cowboy, you're an Indian Bang, bang, wash your face!'

Before he could stop her she'd aimed her toy pistol at his face and pulled the trigger.

Franz uttered a terrible groan as he felt the searing agony. He heard Storm cry out '*No!*' and then all was pandemonium and pain and darkness shot with stabs of scarlet torture and screams of women and children.

Jules sprang to his feet and dragged Franz's burnt hands away from his eyes. Gaby was crying hysterically, the little red plastic pistol lay on the floor where she had dropped it, some of the contents had been discharged, burning a hole in the carpet. Jules took one look at his brother-in-law's tormented and distorted face.

'Oh, my God, it's acid! Quick, Kev, help me get him to a wash-basin. The downstairs cloaks'll do.'

Between them Jules and Kevin helped Franz in his blind agony, drenching his burnt face and hands in clear cold water. Magda stood in the doorway wringing her hands. Jules called to her.

'Telephone Sefton, Mag! He's the best eye man in Cape Town. He can meet us at Groote Schuur casualty in twenty minutes from now. If you can't get Sefton try Mayne. Tell him what's happened. These are acid burns – sulphuric acid or something like it. Tell him I say it's very urgent. Kevin, get your car out at once and drive Franz and me to Groote Schuur. There's no time for questions now. Dad'll help me here.'

The Old Man had appeared in the cloakroom, grey-faced and appalled.

It had all happened in a matter of minutes. After the initial burst of confusion everybody at the table had been stunned and then the voice of Storm had risen shrill above the cries of the children and Colleen's attempts to soothe Huddie.

'So you did it again, Gaby! You climbed up on the work-bench and filled your water pistol from Ali's jar in the tool-shed!'

She was boxing Gaby's ears mercilessly while the child yelled in desperation. What terrible thing had happened? Where had the fun gone wrong?

'I didn't, I didn't!' she cried. 'You took my pistol away from me yesterday —'

Through her tears the frantic child saw the grown-ups milling around. Her grandfather was hurrying out to the car with Uncle Jules and Uncle Franz. She heard her mother's dreadful accusations and somewhere her Aunt Magda was talking on the telephone and then the receiver was replaced with a loud click. Gaby felt blows raining onto the sides of her face as her mother's flattened palms beat at her cheeks.

'There and there and there! You disobedient wicked child! You got your pistol out of my bag and sneaked into the tool-shed.'

And then suddenly protective arms were round her and a cool voice spoke over her head.

'Storm, I think you've gone mad. Leave Gaby alone! Whatever happened was a hideous accident.'

The child turned her wet swollen face and buried it in Magda's bosom.

'I didn't fill my pistol with Ali's stuff,' she sobbed. 'It was water from the fountain – just water. After that Mommy took it away from me.'

Old Lettie was weeping into her apron and Phoebe stood tearfully beside her. Elijah had gone to the car with his master.

'What happened?' asked Colleen in a choked voice as she held the sobbing Huddie on her lap. 'I don't understand, Mag.'

Magda said quietly, 'Somebody filled Gaby's water pistol with acid and Franz received it in his face and eyes when she shot at him.' She turned her head as her father came into the room. 'I've got Sefton, Daddy. He's going straight to Groote Schuur. He'll meet Jules and Franz in the Casualty Department.'

Storm sat with her face buried in her hands. She did not move when they heard the car rev up as Kevin roared down the drive between the gums.

The Old Man nodded. He stood like a rock beside Magda and Gaby as if to protect them from Storm. He stared down at Storm's bowed head, his face grim and accusing. 'I'm going to telephone Dave,' he said. 'It may take some time.'

She looked up. 'So you know! You *do* know where he is. I was right all along.' She threw back her head glaring at him, all her hatred naked in her eyes. He met her gaze steadily.

'We'll talk about that later. There's a lot to be accounted for. At this moment I am going to get hold of Warren Keller, Dave's lawyer, and we'll find out how and where we can contact Dave.'

In Perth the Collins' Christmas party was at its height when the emergency call came through soon after midnight. Mrs Collins answered the phone.

'Cape Town – wanting Mr Davis?' she repeated after the exchange. 'Yes, he's here. Hold on and I'll fetch him.'

'Dave!' she called, as she hurried onto the terrace where he was dancing with Philippa. 'Cape Town wants you on the phone. Christmas greetings, I expect.'

But he blanched as he left Phil and ran to the telephone. No one, except Warren Keller, knew where to find him. What had happened? This could only be bad news. He heard the exchange's voice.

'Mr Davis? Mr Davis . . . your father is coming through from Cape Town . . .'

'Dave —'

'Yes, Dad.'

'Dave, I have shocking news for you. Little Gaby was playing with a toy water pistol after Christmas dinner today. She emptied it into Franz's face and it was filled with acid. We don't know exactly how it happened or why, but he has been badly burnt and we aren't even sure if his eyes can be saved.'

Dance music made a faint mocking background to the sickening words.

'Oh, my God! Who's to blame?'

'We don't know that either. Franz was only taken to hospital an hour ago. There's been no time to investigate the circumstances.'

'I'll be on the next plane, Dad. Is he in danger?'

'Not his life, but his eyes. We haven't got the medical opinion yet.'

Phil was at Dave's side, her eyes wide with horror. The Old Man's grating voice came through with frightening clarity. Dave said:

'I'll be at Blue Horizon as soon as it's humanly possible. I'll cable you my flight number – all details.'

'Do that, my boy.'

'Dad,' said Dave. 'Somehow – God knows why – I feel responsible. I don't know what to say.'

'We don't know the full story yet. By the time you arrive everything will be clearer. Goodbye for now. One of us will be there to meet you.'

Dave hung up and turned to Philippa. They were alone in the study.

'You heard that, Phil. Franz may have been blinded. Acid shot into his face from a child's water pistol. No one knows whose fault it was – but I . . .'

'You think it's Storm.' She was white-faced. She looked as if she might faint, but he scarcely noticed her. He said:

'Why should Storm hurt Franz? Why should anyone harm my brother? If it had been my father I would have blamed Storm. But Franz!'

'Franz – possibly disfigured with his eyes in danger. I can't seem to grasp it.' Her voice was low and shaky.

'Phil,' he said. 'I must ring up the airport now. There

should be a Qantas flight tomorrow morning. I could be home by tomorrow night.'

'Yes,' she said. 'There's no time to waste.'

Hector Morley put the receiver carefully into its cradle and went back to the dining-room with Magda. Colleen had taken the children outside but Storm still sat where he had left her. Elijah and Lettie had cleared the table but no one had touched the little red plastic pistol lying on the floor. Hector took his folded white handkerchief out of his pocket and picked it up carefully.

'The police may want fingerprints,' he said.

'The police?' said Storm, raising her head.

'We don't know for certain that this is a case for the police,' said Hector. 'It may be. That will be decided later. What we need to know now is how acid got into the pistol.'

His leathery features were drawn and his tone was gritty.

'Mag,' he went on. 'I leave it to you to tell the family and the staff that not one word of this disaster is to be mentioned until I give permission. Whether we call in the police or not will rest with me. I will leave the pistol in the top middle drawer of my desk just as it is, wrapped in my handkerchief. I shall need you with me, Magda. You must tell Lettie to take care of your baby during the next couple of hours.' He turned to his daughter-in-law, who was watching him tensely. 'Storm, Magda and I will go home with you and your children. I have some questions to ask you – and to ask Gaby.'

She said, 'I'll fetch Gaby and Garth and Phoebe. We'll meet you at the house.'

'No,' he said. 'Magda will follow with your family and Phoebe in my car. I will go with you in yours.'

Her lips tightened but she did not argue. One look at the Old Man's face forbade resistance.

As she drove him to her home he thought with bitter satisfaction that at least now she could not brief Gaby and put her up to a story of some sort. He meant to get at the truth and wringing that out of Storm might not be easy. The main interrogation would take place in her house but there'd be no harm in putting the wind up her in the meantime.

Storm glanced at the profile of her father-in-law and saw in it the aggressive vigour he seemed to have lost after his wife's death. It was a face battened down for action, strong, inexorable, primed for the final battle against this woman who had brought calamity to his family. Storm decided to take the initiative.

'What did you mean by saying this might be a police case?'

'Someone – and it wasn't Gaby – acted with intent to do grievous bodily harm.'

'Rubbish. It was a horrible accident. Who would want to harm Franz – dear Franz?'

'No one. That acid was not intended for Franz.'

'What makes you say such a thing?'

'I haven't forgotten that you threatened me, Storm, and that you are a woman capable of carrying out your threats.'

'I said I'd pay you out – it's a child's expression and I used it when I was in a rage. It has no significance.'

'In view of what's happened it has the greatest possible significance. I saw the whole incident. You took the toy pistol from your bag and gave it to Gaby and you whispered to her. She looked at me mischievously and she was on her way to me when Franz caught hold of her dress and stopped her. She turned her water pistol on him instead of me and you cried out "No!"'

'I have a quick temper and I talk out of turn. That doesn't mean I'd really try to do you an injury. And after it happened you telephoned Dave. You knew where he was. You knew it all the time.'

'I didn't know where Dave was. I got his address from his lawyer – from Warren Keller. I was lucky to find Keller in.'

'Where was Dave?'

'In Western Australia. He'll fly home as soon as possible and when I say home I mean to Blue Horizon.'

Storm turned into her drive. Magda, in the Old Man's car with Gaby, Garth and Phoebe, followed.

'Now,' said Hector as he got out. 'Let Phoebe take the children out while you and Magda and I have a talk. Afterwards we'll get Gaby's story.'

Hector saw that the sitting-room was garlanded with Christmas cards and in the corner was a Christmas tree sparkling with tinsel and coloured geegaws. Two empty red net stockings were crumpled at its base on the cotton wool sprinkled with silver dust – 'snow' in mid-summer – and so were the gay gilded paper and crisp bows that had wrapped Christmas presents.

'Even with the father away one does one's best.' Storm made a gesture indicating the tree. Beyond the French doors they could see Ali, the Malay, crouched over the slates carefully erasing the last overflow of cement.

'Who's that – working on Christmas Day?' asked Magda.

'The Malay who's been laying the crazy paving of the patio. He only observes Moslem holidays. As you can see, he's using acid for cleaning up the cement between the slates.' Storm turned to Hector. 'You might want a word with Ali. I'm afraid that's where Gaby got the acid.'

'In a minute.' Hector sat down and motioned towards a chair. 'We'll talk here first.'

'Ali knocks off at five,' said Storm stubbornly. 'It's past four now.'

'Magda,' said the Old Man. 'Go and ask Ali not to leave before we have talked to him. He'll no doubt wait to get his money in any case.'

Storm sat on the divan, her legs tucked under her, and lit a cigarette. She looked tired and shaken. Phoebe had taken Gaby for a walk with Garth in his push-cart. The little boy was happily oblivious of the reasons for his sister's small pale face, washed of its tear stains but still wan and heavy lidded, very different from the exuberance she had displayed a few hours earlier.

'There are three things we want to know,' said the Old Man, as Magda rejoined them. 'Why was the water pistol in your bag, Storm? Who filled it with acid? Had Gaby been instructed to aim at a pre-selected victim?'

She said warily; 'I'll answer any questions you want to ask. If this has to be an inquisition you may require a tape recorder. Dave left one here. It's a big one. We use it for taping records-background music.' Her tone was sarcastic and she was astounded when the Old Man took her up on the suggestion.

'An excellent idea. Please produce it.'

She made a gesture of bored and irritated assent and opened a cupboard next to the fireplace.

When the machine was in readiness she sat near it facing Hector. Magda heard the faint hum as the tape began to wind from one roller onto the other.

'Go ahead,' said Storm laconically.

The Old Man's eyes in his worn and furrowed face were deeply concentrated.

'When did Gaby get the water pistol? Who gave it to her?'

'She got it a few weeks ago ... when Ali was first working on the slates. A boy at school gave it to her.'

'Did she play with it much?'

'Yes. She was mad about it. She used to fill it from the fountain. But when Moses was spraying the roses she wanted to fill it from his can of spray but luckily Ali saw her and stopped her in time. Then yesterday she tried to fill it with the acid he was using for the cement. He scolded her and warned me to keep an eye on her. He'll bear me out. Gaby knows she is only allowed to put water in it, so I punished her.'

'How did you punish her?'

'I took the pistol away from her.'

'Yesterday. On Christmas Eve?'

'That's right.'

'How do you account for the acid in the pistol?'

'Ali was working with the acid yesterday morning, as I told you. Gaby always hangs around him when he's working. He tells her stories, he's very good with children. She had the pistol with her. You know how a child clings to some special toy and she adored this beastly thing and was watering the roses with it and wouldn't let it out of her sight. Well,

she wanted to fill it with the acid and spray the cement between the tiles – to help Ali, she said.'

'Like she wanted to help the gardener spray the roses?'
asked Magda.

'Exactly. And, of course, Ali ordered her not to touch the
acid jar and explained to her that it burns.' Storm covered
her face and gasped, 'Oh, Franz – poor Franz . . .'

'It's too late for that sort of thing now,' said the Old Man
implacably. 'Go on with your story.'

'When I came out onto the patio Ali immediately told me
about the incident and that was when I took the pistol from
Gaby. She was very upset and I promised to give it back to
her today – on Christmas Day – on condition that she was a
good girl.'

'You did so. We all saw you.'

'Yes, after lunch, as you know. When the children were
given permission to go out and play I thought she ought to
have it and that she could use it in the garden. We all know
the rest only too well.'

'What we don't know is how the acid got into the pistol.
Have you any theory?'

'When I took the toy from her Gaby saw me put it in my
bag so she knew where to find it. She also knew where Ali
kept the acid. On the shelf in the tool-shed. She must have
sneaked the pistol out of my bag at some time and filled it
and put it back again.'

'Is the tool-shed kept locked?'

'Yes. But the key hangs on the board outside the kitchen
with the garage key and the back door key and one or two
others. She knows them all. She's very intelligent. I don't
have to tell you that.'

'Is she often deliberately disobedient? I shouldn't have thought so myself.'

'She's often naughty and wilful – and she doesn't always tell the truth.'

'You're always very strict with her, Storm. I've had the impression at times that she's afraid of you. Would she really dare to do something you'd expressly forbidden her to do?'

'What else is one to think?'

'What else indeed?' grated Hector significantly. He looked at her intently. 'I should have thought the behaviour you've suggested would require more cunning and follow-through than would be possible or likely in any five-year-old.'

'She's turned six. And she's highly intelligent, as I've just said.'

'Well six years old then, intelligent or not. The bag, the key, the jar, and no error, no spilling of the acid. How could she do all that successfully and undetected?'

Storm shrugged and the Old Man rose.

'What are you trying to imply?' asked Storm.

'Never mind that for the present. Come with us. We'll go and talk to Ali.'

The Malay workman was just packing up his tools. He tipped his fez deferentially as the Old Man addressed him. They gravely exchanged the compliments of the season and then Hector began to put his questions. They spoke in Afrikaans, the language of the Malays and the coloured people. Hector gave a brief explanation for he knew very well that Phoebe would never be able to hold her tongue. The story would get out and he would do well to spread his version first. Storm sat on a garden chair and Magda stood stiffly beside her father.

'Well now, Ali, let's see if you can help us. You know the little girl, Miss Gaby, and you know she had a water pistol? Yes, well, somehow it was filled with acid and the child playfully discharged it into her uncle's face today and burnt it. He's in hospital now. We want to know how she got the acid into the pistol.'

Ali's horrified face twisted. 'This acid can blind a man, sir!'

'I know. But did the child know?'

'I tell her so. She loves that pistol and is always playing with it, pretending to water the flowers. Sometimes she turns it on me and says "Wash your face". Once she tries to fill it with the gardener's insecticide, and only yesterday she wants to fill it from my jar here. I warn her of the danger and I warn Madam too. Madam takes the pistol away. But they all play with it first – Madam and Miss Gaby and the little boy. They fill it from the fountain and squirt the water in each others faces. Madam is laughing, not cross like sometimes. She says "Cowboys and Indians" and "Wash your face!"'

'Was the pistol empty when Madam took it away?'

'How can I say? Miss Gaby filled it at the fountain more than once while they play.'

'Did she know where you kept the acid?'

'Ag, ja.' He smiled. 'She follows me about like a puppy. She is interested in everything. She likes watching me cut the slates to size and mix cement – everything. She's often in and out of the tool-shed where I keep my things.'

'But this acid jar? Surely it was on a shelf out of her reach?'

The man's face fell. 'Ja, it was on a shelf, but she can get to it by climbing onto the workbench. I never think she'll try to do such a thing or fill her pistol from it – not after I warn her.'

'The shed was locked when you left?'

'Before I go I lock the shed and hang the key on the board outside the kitchen. But she knows that, she is a very clever child. She notices everything.'

'Could anyone else have filled the pistol?'

Ali's almond eyes grew wary. 'How can I say? When last I see the pistol Madam is putting it away in her bag.'

'What about the little boy, Garth?' asked Magda.

The Malay smiled. 'Ah, no, Madam. He's still too small. Anyway, Miss Gaby don't lend her pistol to nobody. Her brother can yell his head off for it, but she hangs onto it.' He spread his hands to indicate the helplessness of the male confronted with the feminine possessive instinct.

'What will you do with that jar of acid now?' asked Magda.

'It's nearly empty, Madam, and my job is done. I'll throw out these few drops and put the jar with the rubbish.'

'Put it in the boot of my car. I may need it,' said Hector. 'That's all for the present, Ali. If I want to speak to you again where can I find you?'

'Madam knows my address, sir. So does Phoebe. Moses too. There is no difficulty. I'll put the jar in a bit of old sacking.'

'You won't find my fingerprints on it – if that's what you're thinking,' Storm burst out suddenly and viciously.

The Old Man turned and stared at her long and hard.

'We won't find Gaby's either, I imagine. Gaby would hardly think of wearing gloves if she were going to steal

acid. It's my belief she never touched that jar.' He took a
bunch of keys from his pocket and handed them to Magda.

'Here's the key to the boot, Mag. This one. When Ali has
put the jar away, please rejoin us.'

He observed the quick flush that suffused Storm's apricot
skin and subsided, leaving her outwardly calm, but there
were drops of moisture on her forehead and upper lip although the heat of the day had long since abated and the late
afternoon was fresh. He indicated that she should follow him
into the house, leaving Magda with Ali. Phoebe had returned
with the children and was bathing them.

'They have supper in their dressing-gowns,' said Storm.
'When do you want to interrogate Gaby?' She used the
word 'interrogate' with a bitter inflection and a curl of her
lip.

'I'll see her now. Alone. Here by this useful tape recorder
of yours.'

'I'll send her down to you,' she said.

'No,' he put in quickly. 'I'll fetch her myself.'

But Gaby was already in the doorway in her little white
dressing-gown with its sprigs of rosebuds. Her chestnut
curls had been brushed till they gleamed and her well
scrubbed face was pale but no longer swollen and blotched
with tears.

'You evidently want me out of the way,' said Storm.

'Go to your son,' said Hector, 'and keep him in the nursery
until I give the all clear. Gaby and I are going to have a quiet
chat all by ourselves.'

'With your silent witness.' Storm cast a disdainful glance
at the tape recorder. 'Can you work it by yourself?'

'I can turn a switch on and off with the best of them.'

He watched her go and then he took the child on his knee and she squirmed off. 'Let me turn the switch!'

'Of course, if you want to.'

There was the faint hum in the room once more and the twitter of birds outside as the little girl climbed back onto her grandfather's lap.

'Are you going to tell me a story?' she asked.

'No, sweetheart, not yet. Later maybe I will. First I want to ask you something.'

Fear and guilt leapt into her eyes. 'About my water pistol?'

'Yes.'

'I didn't – I didn't! I never put Ali's stuff in it. I wanted to, but he wouldn't let me. Then Mommy came and scolded me and took it away from me. But we all played with it first. She squirted it in my eyes and said "Wash your face", and I cried. But Garth didn't cry. It was only a game.'

'All that was yesterday?'

'Mmn,' she nodded. 'Before supper.'

'Then your Mommy put it in her bag?'

'Mmn. But first I filled it at the fountain. Not from Ali's stuff – only from the fountain.'

'So today, when she gave it back to you after dinner, you thought it was full of water?'

'Mmn.'

'And whose face were *you* going to wash?'

She snuggled against his chest. 'You'll be cross,' she mumbled.

'I won't be cross. Nobody is cross on Christmas Day.'

'That's what Mommy said – but Mommy was cross. Mommy smacked me and smacked me —'

'I won't be cross. And I won't smack you. Tell me now.

Was it *my* face you were going to wash? Were you coming to play your splashing games with me?'

She nodded vigorously.

'Why did you choose me, sweetheart?'

'Mommy told me to. Mommy said you wouldn't be cross. She dared me.'

'*She dared you?*'

"Cos I was scared you'd be cross. So she dared me.'

'And when your Uncle Franz caught hold of your dress you changed your mind?'

'Mmn . . .'

He felt her begin to shake in his arms and a sob broke from her. He held her more tightly against him, stroking her curls very gently.

'It wasn't your fault, my little one. It was an accident. Uncle Franz will get better. And later we'll throw the old pistol away. Pistols aren't good toys for little girls. I'm taking care of yours for now. Don't cry, sweetheart. No one is angry with you any more and soon your Daddy will be coming home.'

She clung to him. 'I'm frightened of Mommy. She'll beat me with the hairbrush.'

'She won't beat you with anything, I promise you. I'm going to take you and Garth back to Blue Horizon with me now – to keep me company. And when your Daddy comes home won't that be the best Christmas present of all? In the meantime we're all going to be at Blue Horizon. You and Garth can sleep in the little pink room near Huddie and Pam. You'll like that, won't you?'

'Will Mommy come too?'

'I think not,' he said. 'But Phoebe will.'

A thin warning bell rang and there was a buzzing sound from the tape recorder.

'Look, the tape's all finished,' said Hector. 'I'll turn it off.'

'Let me Gran'pa!'

'Good, you do it then.'

She scrambled off his lap and threw the switch and the little bell ceased ringing and there was no more buzzing. It was very quiet in the room. But three words echoed in the Old Man's ears – '*She dared me.*'

10

THE FAMILY

FRANZ LAY IN A CUBICLE AT THE END OF A LONG
ward bright with Christmas decorations. But all was darkness for him as his eyes were swathed in bandages. The first
appalling agony of that endless afternoon had been soothed
by a pain killing injection, and now he was reasonably comfortable although he felt muzzy and confused and the world
beyond his hospital cot had been reduced to a place of sensation and sound alone – the touch of a nurse's hand, the stab of
a needle, the taste of clear tea, rumble of a trolley, swish of
traffic taking the Hospital Curve round Devil's Peak, doves
cooing in the pines on the mountainside, and tugs hooting
in the bay. He tried to control the claustrophobia of the
bandages, the suspense of wondering what damage had been
done, and the endless procession of vague frightening images
wandering across the screen of his mind – a passing parade
of faint hopes and hideous fears. What when the bandages
were removed? Blindness perhaps. Disfigurement? People
trying to keep their voices normal when they spoke to him.
'It's not too bad really – a scar or two . . .' Already Sefton
had assured him that there was 'nothing wrong that a little
plastic surgery' couldn't put right, but the surgeon had made
no promise about the exact degree of sight that would be
restored.

'Might I be blind?' Franz had asked.

'I shouldn t think on those lines if I were you,' Sefton had replied easily. 'In a little while we'll be better able to assess the whole situation.'

His hearing had intensified during the past few hours and he felt his body tense as he caught the familiar slightly halting step and deep weary voice of his father asking the staff nurse if they might go in. Kevin was with him.

'Yes,' she said. 'It's visiting time – seven to seven-thirty.' Then they were walking the length of the ward to his cubicle and the nurse was at his bedside. 'Your father and brother to see you, Mr Morley. Let them do the talking. The stiller you keep your face the better.'

Franz said, 'Hallo, Dad. Hallo, Kev.' There were burns along his right cheekbone and his lips felt stiff.

The nurse's step receded and he was aware of the brief touch of his father's hand on his wrist, cold with age in spite of the summer's heat. They greeted him casually, any emotion they might have felt carefully controlled. His father said:

'It's I who should be lying here, not you. She meant that acid for me and you took a risk when you intercepted Gaby. You were very quick to realize something was up.'

'I only tried to save you a douche of cold water.'

'That's as maybe. We've discovered where the acid came from. A Malay workman was using it to clean up the cement between the slate paving on Storm's new patio. Somebody filled the pistol from his container.'

'Little Gaby?'

'That's what Storm would like us to believe,' said the Old Man grimly. 'It seems she confiscated the child's pistol and put it in her bag before Ali put the acid jar away in the toolshed. She only returned it to Gaby after Christmas dinner, as you know. Gaby meant to shoot me for a joke. She thought it was filled with water.'

'Is Gaby all right?' asked Franz.

'Both children are at Blue Horizon where we can keep an eye on them,' said Kevin. 'Storm is in her own home. We expect Dave back tomorrow night about nine-thirty.' He hesitated for a moment as though he wanted to add something, but Hector shook his head and put a finger across his lips. Before Franz could speak the Old Man cut in and explained how he and Magda had gone to Storm's house and spoken to Ali and how they had questioned both mother and child.

'What now?' asked Franz when he had heard the whole story.

'After Dave arrives and we've had a chance of discussing things with him I shall tell the assembled family exactly what has happened and what our conclusions are.'

'It's not going to be easy to find the answers.'

'We'll find them,' said Hector firmly. 'We must sift all the evidence and decide with Dave what is best for him and the children. For Storm too. And then we must go ahead with whatever plan we think best.'

'What about the farm – about Golden Grass?' Franz asked. 'They expect me back the day after tomorrow.'

'I've telephoned Pierre Malan,' said Kevin. 'He'll hold the fort until you're well. And I'll be going back to Johannesburg soon. I'll drive out there and make sure everything's right.'

The staff nurse was ringing her little hand-bell. Time for visitors to leave. Suddenly Franz said:

'How did you get hold of Dave? Where was he?'

'In Western Australia,' said the Old Man stonily. 'As you

know, it's a long flight home. Warren Keller told me where I could contact him.'

'Exactly where was that?' Pinpoint it, know for sure what he'd already guessed. As his father answered, Franz uttered an involuntary groan.

'In the home of Mr Jim Collins of Perth. He was spending Christmas with the Collins family – the same ones you knew so well. We must go now. The second bell has rung. You'll be seeing . . . well, Jules will be in to see you later. He's a doctor and he can disregard the hospital rules.'

'So long, old boy,' said Kevin. 'Mag and Colleen send love. Only two of us are allowed to come at a time, or they'd have been here. Be sure we'll keep you in the picture, whatever happens.'

'Goodbye,' said Franz, exhausted and aching in body and mind.

As they left him and the last footsteps of friends and relatives faded and the ward grew quiet, the old familiar adolescent jealousy flared up in him again. His brother and his girl. So Dave had spent Christmas with Phil as he, Franz, had hoped to do a year ago? So Dave must have been seeing her and getting to know her all these past months. Falling in love with her, no doubt. What had decided Dave to choose Western Australia as his hiding place from Storm, anyway? Franz remembered that he had told his brother about Mr Collins and his mining interests in the north-west. Had he used that knowledge to seek a job of some sort? Probably, yes. He was a born opportunist, clever and enterprising. It was obvious too that he would have changed his name and kept his identity and his whereabouts secret so that Storm should be unable to trace him. Perth was the nearest

Australian city to Cape Town. He'd have tried his luck there
and he'd have found some way of approaching the one man
he knew might help him – Jim Collins, the mining magnate.
He must inevitably have met Phil, who would have noticed
the striking resemblance between Dave and the man who
had been her lover. Her interest would naturally have been
aroused. Franz knew only too well how attractive his
brother was to women. He stifled a deep sigh.

Confused as he was, he realized that his imagination was
running away with him. What good was it to lie here in the
dark painting his own tormenting pictures of events that bore
little relation to fact? He told himself that Phil wasn't Dave's
type. Storm was. Pain began to mount in him, the pain of
his burns and his memories and his sense of loss. His fingers
tightened on the little round bell-push the nurse had left
under his hand.

'Ring if the pain gets too tough,' she had said. 'We can
give you another injection.'

He'd ring right now. Anything for oblivion.

Dusk had fallen over the wide highveld when the Qantas
jet prepared to land at Johannesburg on Boxing Day. The
sunset had been theatrical and the afterglow still bathed the
grasslands. Summer storms played along far horizons, threatening a bumpy ride. Dave looked at his watch.

'Not much time to make that seven-thirty-five Cape Town
connection. We're running late.'

Phil said: 'I almost hope we miss it. I've got butterflies
in my tummy. I must have been mad to come.'

'You were dead right to come. Fasten your seat belt.'

When she had obeyed him, he took her hand and held it

tightly and did not release it until the wheels had touched down on the runway.

The Customs were brisk, the black porter handled their luggage efficiently and they were on board the south-bound aircraft in the minimum of time. The air hostess made her little welcoming speech in English and Afrikaans, dinner was served as soon as they were airborne and Phil looked down at the vast darkening Karoo and thought that, after all, South Africa was not unlike Australia. Then the Cape mountains rose in range upon range under the stars and Dave said:

'Soon we'll be there.'

'I'm scared of your father,' she said. 'I'm scared of all your family, but most of all I'm scared of meeting Franz again.'

'Blame everything on me. I've done so much harm already —'

'Hush,' she said. 'Self-reproach won't get you anywhere.'

A tall hawk-faced man with spectacles met them at the barrier. He greeted his brother with a slap on the back, and Dave introduced him to Phil. 'My brother, Kevin, Philippa Collins.'

Kevin smiled and Phil, who had thought at first that he looked forbidding, relaxed.

'You've come a long way to meet Dave's family,' he said. 'Welcome.'

'How is Franz?' she asked.

'We won't know the prognosis till tomorrow. There's to be a consultation in the afternoon.'

'When will it be possible to see him?' asked Dave.

'Not till tomorrow evening, I'm afraid. Visiting hours are seven to seven-thirty and they're pretty strict.'

Hector Morley and Colleen were on the doorstep to meet them at Blue Horizon, and, as soon as the greetings and introductions were over, Dave said:

'The children, where are they?'

'Upstairs, asleep,' said Hector. 'We didn't tell them you were arriving tonight or they'd have been too excited to close their eyes. Tomorrow will do.'

But Colleen took Dave's arm. 'Come up and peep at them. No need to wake them.'

'You come too, Phil,' said Dave.

The curtains and windows were open and the slatted teak outer shutters were on the hook. A shaft of moonlight fell across the space between the two beds. The landing light shone through the open door and Phil saw the two heads on the white pillows – the boy's hair dark and tangled. He had kicked off his coverings and he lay on his back with his hands flung wide. The girl's face was buried in her pillow as if she might have cried herself to sleep.

Dave drew the sheet gently over his son, who did not stir, then he went to the other bed where he touched Gaby's chestnut curls with his lips. She made a slight movement but did not wake.

'Poor little thing,' he whispered.

Colleen nodded. 'Jules gave her a tablet to make her sleep. She's terribly overwrought. But she'll be all right, given time. There's no real guilt. She didn't mean to do any harm.'

As they went downstairs for a cup of coffee Dave asked about Storm.

'She's in her own home,' said Colleen.

'I don't intend to see her, except in the presence of Warren Keller,' he said firmly.

While they were drinking their coffee Hector told them all that had happened the day before, as far as he knew it.

'You and I will need to have a long talk tomorrow, Dave,' he said. 'And at five o'clock, after the consultation about Franz, I have arranged a family get-together here. Warren Keller and Storm too, because certain decisions must be taken and put into effect.'

He turned to Phil kindly. 'And now, one thing is sure. Our guest needs a good night's rest. Let Colleen take Phil to her room.'

When Phil woke next morning the sun was shining and her bedside travelling clock told her that it was nearly eleven. She had slept the clock round, exhausted and dreamless.

She sprang out of bed and went to the open window. The beauty of the spring scene was breathtaking. A green lawn with a spreading oak to one side of it and beyond it the rose garden, the blue jacarandas, the sea and the lavender camber of the mountains. Two golden labradors sprawled in the sun and a cat sat on the low wall of the rose garden and washed itself fastidiously. Gaby and Garth and Huddie were playing nosily in the shadow of the tree and Colleen sat nearby, one hand rocking a pram, the other holding a small child in her lap. She glanced up at the window and caught sight of Phil.

'Awake at last!' she called. 'I'll send you some breakfast.'

'It's too late for that,' answered Phil. 'Just a cup of coffee, please.'

'Fine. And then come out here and join us. You must meet the children – our Huddie and Pam, Dave's Garth and Gaby and Magda's Hector here in the pram. Mag's with Dad and Dave in the study where they can have a good pow-wow in peace and quiet.'

Colleen dumped Pam on the grass while she went indoors to order Phil's coffee. 'Keep an eye on Pam, Gaby,' she said, and the little girl responded with bossy self-importance.

When Phil went out onto the lawn half an hour later, feeling rested and refreshed, she found that a tall attractive young woman had joined Colleen and the children. Magda sprinted across the grass to meet her and seized both her hands.

'So you're Phil! We've just been hearing all about you from Dave. It was splendid and brave of you to come here with him.'

Phil wanted to laugh and cry at the genuine warmth of Magda's welcome.

'It was crazy of me,' she said. 'But when I heard what had happened here it shocked me into a sudden . . . a sort of . . . self-knowledge. I simply had to come You know, of course, that I've let Franz down very badly. I have to see him and explain everything to him – as soon as possible.'

Magda said quietly, 'He doesn't yet know you're here. We thought it best not to tell him till after the consultation – till we know how bad things are. He's been through a great deal, Phil. I doubt if you quite understand all the implications.'

'I think I do. Franz may lose his sight.'

Magda looked at Phil with sympathy. 'In which case, it might be best if you don't see him at all. He'd be very sensitive to . . . pity.'

'I must see him, whatever happens. I'm sorry, but that's how it is. Dave understands.'

Magda stole a glance at the strong stubborn young face and shrugged her shoulders.

'As you like. Jules will take you to the hospital this evening. In the meantime come and meet this rabble of infants.'

During the next few hours Phil found it difficult to stave off the veiled but searching interest of Magda and Colleen. They were jumping to conclusions about her and as yet she was unable to satisfy their curiosity. It seemed to her that she was losing confidence by the minute. Her overwhelming impulse to fly to South Africa with Dave now appeared absurd and even impertinent. Here was a family in desperate trouble – Dave holding himself responsible for a ghastly accident – or plot – and Franz cruelly injured – Franz, who had once been so confident of her love and courage and whom she had failed. But they were kind and friendly and seemed anxious to make her feel at home. Dave, haggard and disturbed, still managed to be reassuring.

'Don't lose your nerve, darling. Everything will be all right. Jules has just phoned from the hospital that the report on Franz is better than anyone dared hope. He'll be here any time now – Jules, I mean.'

It was nearly five o'clock, time for the family conference.

'You'll come in with me,' said Dave, when she demurred. 'Everything that concerns us concerns you too – my situation, Franz's —'

'But your father —

'Dad understands. I put him wise to everything this morning. Naturally he appreciates that nothing can be said for the time being. He's deeply touched by the fact that you came at all.'

Phil went with Dave into the long sitting-room where old Hector Morley was already seated behind a table facing his audience with a big fair man at his side who was introduced to her as Jules Strauss, Magda's husband. She thought he looked tired and stern but the sort of person you'd trust. Dave led her to a seat between Magda and himself. Kevin and Colleen sat on the couch and a little apart from them was a beautiful woman with red-gold hair and defensive eyes as hard as jewels. She sat on a high-backed winged chair and next to her was an owlish bald-headed man with a narrow disapproving mouth.

'Storm and Warren Keller, my solicitor,' Dave murmured to Phil, his face tense. Storm was staring at him with a questioning resentful face. The solicitor nodded briefly.

Hector rose. His light Palm Beach suit hung loosely on his shoulders even when he braced them as he did now. It was clear that he intended to conduct this meeting in his own way and that he had the authority to do so. Only Storm dared to flaunt it. She said boldly from her chair:

'You are putting the case for the prosecution, I presume, Mr Morley. And you have appointed yourself both judge and jury.'

The Old Man looked down at her.

'I shall sum up the events of Christmas Day as they appear to me, but anyone here who disagrees with my assessment has every right to say so and his or her opinion will be heard and considered. If we can handle this sad business among ourselves there will be no need to call in the police. I hope we can but that will depend on you, Storm. I must insist, however, that everything said in this room today shall be regarded as absolutely confidential.' His gaze was directed at Warren Keller who nodded assent.

Storm's face hardened. She had her back to the wall but she was not beaten yet. She took a cigarette from the case in her leopard-skin handbag and Keller gave her a light. She wore a plain yellow linen dress with a leopard-skin belt. She was less made up than usual but her tawny hair shone and the flush on her cheekbones heightened the glitter of her yellow eyes.

She looks dangerous, thought Phil, and terribly attractive in her own blatant exotic way. No wonder she had held Dave in the hollow of her hand. But, looking at her, Dave knew that the old magnetism would never again stir his blood. He waited for his father to open the case against his wife.

THE DARK AND THE DAWN

'JULES HAS SOMETHING TO TELL US,' HECTOR SAID. 'He has come straight here from Groote Schuur Hospital.'

He sat down and Jules stood up and straightened his back deliberately. He spoke gravely but with obvious relief.

'I have good news for you. We held a consultation about Franz this afternoon and Sefton and Mayne are agreed that it will be possible to save most of his sight. As regards the burns, a certain amount of plastic surgery will be needed for that, but it shouldn't be extensive. Luckily he turned his head away instinctively when Gaby raised the water pistol and most of the contents affected only the right half of the forehead and the right cheek and a small part of the neck. We can assume that although he will be scarred he won't be disfigured any more than a duellist is disfigured by the scar of a blade.'

There was a murmur of relief and faces cleared. Phil felt tears prick her eyes and even Storm stirred and bowed her head as if in gratitude. Jules sat down and the Old Man was once more on his feet.

'For that verdict at least we can be thankful, but Franz still has to face surgery and suffering, and the guilt for that lies squarely upon Storm.'

'It was an accident,' she said in a low obstinate voice. 'You know that. The child was at fault.'

Hector turned to her. 'That Franz was hurt was indeed an accident. The acid was intended for me, and I mean to exonerate Gaby absolutely. You told me once you didn't do your dirty work yourself. You proved that on Christmas Day when you made a cat's paw of your innocent child —'

'That's a lie!'

'I will prove it to the contrary. Let me go back a bit.'

He addressed his family now. His eyes sought Dave's and then looked away again.

'When Dave decided to leave Storm he came to me. He asked me for temporary financial assistance. When he had satisfied me that it was no longer possible for him to live with his wife, I helped him. But I refused to allow him to tell me where he planned to go. Only Warren Keller, our solicitor, knew that. We were, as you know, able to communicate with Dave through Warren. I'm going to ask Dave to tell you frankly why he felt compelled to leave his wife as the final straw has an important bearing on certain decisions we have reached about the future. Dave knows exactly what happened on Christmas Day, as you all do. I have told him everything.'

Storm turned her head and looked full at Dave with something like a plea in her eyes. He faced her in a quiet forceful manner, his habitual restless movements disciplined like the guarded tone of his voice. He addressed himself to her, coldly and dispassionately.

'You were furious, Storm, because my father refused to pay for the luxuries you wanted. What I could give you didn't satisfy you. But you refused to divorce me because you still hoped to lay hands on my share of the Trust at Dad's death. On the evening of my mother's funeral we quarrelled and you admitted that Sidney Barralet had died because you had withheld the tablets he most desperately needed for his heart condition.' He paused and allowed the words to sink in. A gasp of horror breathed through the quiet room. Phil thought, it can't be true, nobody could be so cruel and pitiless! No wonder Dave couldn't live with such terrible knowledge. Storm cried out:

'You've made that up. You can't prove any such thing.'

'I can't prove it,' said Dave. 'It's your word against mine. But you know it's true – mercilessly true. That's why I couldn't live with you any longer. When I realized the truth I deserted you and hoped that you would want to divorce me sooner or later. I still hope that.'

She half rose, gripping the arms of her chair with white knuckles as she flung her counter accusation into the taut silence of the room.

'So you fled as far as you could go – to Australia. Yet you trusted your son and your step-daughter to me! I was good enough for that! Would you really have done that if you had believed me to be a murderess? I deny that I told you anything about Sidney Barralet's death. It was natural. I had no hand in it.'

Dave ignored her outburst. He continued steadily. 'Before I left, my father asked me for my assurance that the children would be safe in your care. I gave it to him. I could never have believed that even you would use a child – your own daughter – to lure her into committing a horrible crime without the least idea of what she was doing or why she was doing it. I take the blame for being such a fool. I should have realized that nothing was beyond you.'

'It was an accident, I tell you. Gaby stole the pistol from

my bag to fill it with Ali's acid and she put it back in my bag. She's clever and sly. She likes to play with dangerous things – like insecticide or acid.'

'Gaby would never have disobeyed you so flagrantly. *She was afraid of you* and Dad had the acid jar tested for finger-prints. Only Ali's were on it. You, no doubt, wore gloves when you took off the lid to fill the pistol. You would have worn them so as not to burn yourself, wouldn't you?'

Hector had risen. He made a sign to Dave to sit down.

'When Storm came to see me after Dave had disappeared she was under the impression that I was responsible for his desertion. She threatened me. She said she would have her revenge, that she would pay me out. On Christmas Day, when she gave Gaby back the water pistol, she dared the child to shoot it at me. *She dared Gaby*. What child doesn't respond to a dare? In all innocence Gaby ran round the table towards me and only by chance did Franz avert her and suffer the vengeance intended for me.'

Magda put in: 'We have a tape recording of the conversation between Storm and Dad after the event and of the talk between Dad and little Gaby. You can hear it afterwards if you wish and you'll find it conclusive. Those words of Gaby's – "She dared me!" – tell the whole dreadful story.'

'Why didn't Storm do it herself?' asked Colleen sharply. 'Why put the burden of guilt and horror on a mere child?'

Storm stared at her in sullen silence. The high colour had drained out of her face and she was deathly pale. Jules glanced at her with a frown. She was a dangerous animal, cornered and at bay. He rose and said:

'Storm wanted to make it appear an accident. Failing that,

she counted on the Morley family unity and pride to safe-guard her. She knew the reluctance any one of us would feel to call in the police and create a major scandal. She risked her child's sanity to save her own skin and to indulge her desire for revenge without taking the consequences. To a certain extent she has succeeded. The family does not want to wash such filthy linen in public. Storm cannot he held responsible for the death of her first husband at this stage. It would be impossible to make such an accusation stick. Nor need she be imprisoned for the grievous bodily harm she has caused Franz Morley. But she can only avoid that last eventuality if she agrees to certain restraints. If she refuses we will call in the police and let official justice take its course.'

Storm's desperate gaze scanned her father-in-law's face. She knew that Gaby's words – recorded on the tape – had condemned her. What a fool she had been to dare the child! And to offer Hector the tape recorder – an impulsive crazy gesture of defiance.

Hector was on his feet. 'I have discussed this matter at length with Dave and Jules and Magda because they are the people most vitally concerned. It appears to us that there are three essential conditions with which Storm must comply. First, she has proved herself unfit to have the care of children. Or of invalids,' he added significantly. Storm shook her head in fierce negation of the implied accusation, but Hector continued. 'Or of any other human being. She must give up all claims to Gaby and Garth and agree never to attempt to see them again. Any court of law would agree. Am I right, Warren?'

'In the circumstances, you are right, Mr Morley,' said Keller. 'If the full facts were known.'

'Garth!' gasped Storm, her face contorted. 'Not Garth. I can't, I won't give up my son.'

The Old Man stared at her grimly. 'You have no alternative. Give him up voluntarily, here and now, or face the police and the public court room and all that the publicity and scandal would mean to you and your children – especially to Gaby – now and later. You will lose both children either way.'

He turned away from her, as if dismissing her plea.

'Secondly, Storm must divorce Dave and leave him free to make a new decent life for himself. He tells me he wishes to settle in Australia and he will no doubt marry again one of these days.'

Storm shot a malevolent glance at Philippa Collins, the girl who had been made welcome by this family.

'Thirdly,' continued Hector, 'she must settle abroad. I will make it financially possible. Then perhaps she too will see the error of her ways and make a new and better start in life. These affairs will be largely arranged at the earliest possible moment.'

'What about my children?' asked Storm. 'What have you planned for them?'

'Magda and Jules will take your children until such time as Dave is able to make a proper home for them. Gaby has been badly shocked and no two people are better qualified to handle her than Magda, who is devoted to her, and whom she adores, and Jules, who is a medical man with a great understanding of children in general and this child in particular.' He turned from Storm to Jules, and then to Dave.

'Jules and Magda are both only too willing to take the

responsibility of the children, and Dave fully agrees. The practical arrangements will be ironed out in detail later.'

'Garth,' persisted Storm desperately. 'Let me keep Garth! For the rest, I'll do as you say.'

'I'm sorry.' The Old Man was not ready to give an inch. 'If there's one streak of good in you, Storm, it's your love for Garth. But he must remain with his sister and be safe.'

She pushed her hair back from her forehead with a demented hand, and, before anyone could stop her, she had sprung up and escaped from the room out into the garden. It was Jules who saw and recognized the grief and near madness in her eyes. He slipped out of his place and caught up with her as she was getting into her car.

'Storm,' he said. 'Wait!'

She was sitting behind the wheel with the long evening shadow of the palm tree across her face.

'I'll come and see you later,' he said. 'We'll discuss the future of the children and your own future. You're a young woman, you can still make good. There are places where you can lead a new life just as Dave is going to do. We can plan something. You can learn from what's happened. It's not too late.'

She looked at him strangely, touched by the compassion in his voice. The wildness gradually left her face and gave way to defeat.

'Does a leopard change its spots? You don't know me at all, Jules. None of you know me. You don't know my father or my mother or my beginnings. You don't understand the rages that shake me. Sometimes I've wondered if I'm . . . quite like other people. My mother died in a home for inebriates. There's violence in our stars. I've done great harm in this family, and I'm bitterly sorry about Franz. It would be easy to love Franz. I'm not incapable of love, you know.'

He looked at her with a glimmer of hope in his eyes. If she could plumb the depths of her own dark side and learn to rise above it there was still a chance for her as a human being. Jules knew a psychiatrist who was also a great humanitarian. This man could surely help Storm. Well, later, he would see if he could persuade her to undergo a course of treatment.

'I know you are capable of love,' he said. 'You love Garth very dearly – better than yourself. Be sure of one thing. Your son will have love and care while he's in our charge. He's a great little fellow. And you know that Gaby is precious to us too.'

'I know, but Garth – oh God!' Her voice broke, but she recovered herself. 'There was a time when I thought I'd learnt the meaning of the word love – the time I first knew and wanted Dave. But that was different. It was only after my son was born that I understood what real love could be ... but I am as I am, and, even for his sake, I didn't succeed in changing myself. I thought the Old Man would fall for Garth and reinstate Dave. But he didn't. He's always discriminated against us – because of me. So I hated him. And when he tempted Dave to leave me and made it possible and covered up for him I ... I just went mad. There was what the lawyers call – provocation.'

'Not for what you did to Gaby,' said Jules, stern again.

She shook her head helplessly and switched on the ignition. Her foot was on the accelerator. As she drove away Jules saw that she had dropped her leopard-skin bag outside the car. He stopped and picked it up and called after her.

'Hey, Storm! Your bag. Stop!' But she was on her way.

He looked down at the bag and touched the spotted fur. It was wet. He realized that while she had been talking to him she had also been weeping.

In the long sitting-room the conference was over. The Old Man, Dave and Warren Keller had retired to the study to discuss business details concerning Storm and her children. Magda and Colleen had gone upstairs to help Phoebe put the little ones to bed and Phil found herself alone with Kevin. The table at which Hector Morley had sat in judgement had been removed, and Phil and Kevin strolled over to the fire-place and looked up at the portrait of Marie Morley.

'Your mother, of course,' said Phil.

'Yes. If she'd been alive none of this would have happened.'

'She has a wonderful face – gay, compassionate and strong.'

'She was quite worldly, in her way. She understood people.' Kevin took off his glasses and polished them with his handkerchief. 'She was the one person who could control Storm. She was always kind to her. She used to say that it was possible to overcome evil with good.'

'But you all tried to do that.'

'Not really. We never let Storm feel that she belonged. Only Mother attempted to do that. Immediately she was gone the fiction that Storm was one of us was destroyed. The rest followed inevitably.'

'I wish I had known your mother.'

'I do too. You would have loved her and she would have respected you. Courage and loyalty meant a great deal to her. I think you have both.'

'Thank you,' said Phil. 'It's taken a tragedy to prove them.'

They turned as Jules came into the room.

'We should be going, Phil. I haven't warned Franz that

you are coming. I thought you might still want to change your mind.'

'I'm ready to come with you now,' she said firmly.

'Good,' he said. 'Then away we go.'

She gave a last glance at the portrait and followed Jules from the room into the warm summer evening with its scent of roses and twitter of birds.

When the visitors' bell rang at seven o'clock and the doors opened Franz listened for the invading footsteps. They surged in like a stream in spate and he tried to distinguish those that would be for him – footsteps that would walk the full length of the ward to his private cubicle at the end. His ears strained for his father's long stride and Dave's crisper tread. Dave would have arrived at Blue Horizon last night. He would have had all day to discuss his future plans and the children's – to see Storm, perhaps – and now he would come to check for himself the harm that had been done. Franz stirred uneasily. It was going to be awkward to meet his brother again. In a way it was Dave's fault that he lay here now with his burnt and damaged eyes. If Dave hadn't married Storm in the face of the family's opposition, if he hadn't deserted her, all this would never have happened. Franz's feelings towards his brother were mixed and turbulent. It had been a shock to him to learn that he had been spending Christmas in the Collins' home. The news had stirred up memories he had tried to bury – the more acutely, he thought, because he lay in the dark looking inwards with nothing to distract his attention from pictures of Phil and the growth of a love he had failed to eradicate. He had written to her once and received no answer, and, after that, he had accepted the finality of the break. Or had he? Had hope lingered on secretly? For all he knew she was Mrs Ian Gray now. Dave could tell him that, at all events. And more. Franz would guess at once, by the tone of his brother's voice, whether Phil had come to mean more than a friend to him. Darkness and pain had made him hypersensitive.

The surge into the ward and the scrape of wooden stools had settled down, giving way to the murmur of voices. Above them Franz heard the tread of a man and a woman approaching his cubicle. The man? Not his father, not Dave. Jules? Yes, Jules. And the woman? He held his breath as the light firm step drew near. Not brisk and purposeful like a nurse's but a step he had heard so many times half a world away. Coming down the path from the School of the Air, crossing the grass at Black Swan, walking at his side to the barrier at Perth Airport on a night of parting that had been, for him, a small death.

'I'm dreaming,' he thought now. The same old unhappy dream that begins with hope and ends with frustration.

Now scent added to the illusion – the light fragrance of loquat flowers in early spring, evoking Menindee Lakes and the eerie drumming of swans in the moonlight.

Jules' voice broke into the dream.

'I've brought a friend to see you, Franz. She's come a very long way and she has a lot to say to you, so I'm going to leave you now and I'll tell Sister to make sure you aren't disturbed. I'll be along some time tomorrow.'

They were alone, the scent closer, more potent. He stretched his unbandaged hand towards her, still unbelieving. He felt her fingers, slim and cool, slide into his palm with a soft intimate pressure, well remembered.

'Hi, Franz!'

'Hi, Phil. I know it's just hallucination – these damn pain-killers. Let's pretend it's real.'

'It's real.'

She raised his hand to her face and held it against her cheek.

'Your cheek is wet.'

She shook her head and did not answer.

'Don't cry, Phil. The doctors came this afternoon. They say I'll get my sight back – most of it, anyhow, and a spot of plastic surgery will make me presentable. Not to worry. What brought you here?'

'I came with Dave. He was staying with us in Perth over Christmas and then he heard this awful thing. Your father telephoned. Dave knew he must get home at once. I came with him.'

Her words tumbled over each other. As he heard them, the feeling of muzziness and brief euphoria left him, and it seemed to him that the old inevitable pattern rose between them. His brother and his girl.

'You wouldn't come with me, but you came with Dave.'

He heard her long indrawn breath and he withdrew his hand gently from hers. They were separate once more. It was easier so.

'What is Dave going to do?'

'There was a family session this afternoon. Dave insisted I should be present though I didn't want to intrude. Storm will divorce him. Your father delivered an ultimatum. Either she gives Dave his freedom or the police will be called in. Jules and Magda will take the children till Dave can make a real home for them.'

'Divorce is quick in this country and the grounds are easy. Desertion, I suppose.'

'I gather so. When the arrangements have been made Dave will fly back to Western Australia. He's working there for Pop – in the iron ore country. You'd be proud of the way he's taken it in the outback – and at its hottest toughest season —'

'So that's how you met him? And now Dave gets his freedom and goes back to your country. You won't have to leave your people. The children will have a sweet new mother —'

'Aren't you jumping to conclusions rather fast?' she interrupted.

'Not really. I think I've guessed this ever since I knew he'd spent Christmas at your home in Perth. Twenty-four hours ago I heard that. So, you see, I've had time to let my imagination run riot. When did you fall in love with him? At first sight?'

'At first sight,' she said, slowly. 'Yes.'

He heard the scrape of the wooden stool as she sat beside him and suddenly he felt her warmth and nearness in every nerve. He put out his hand gropingly and touched her shoulder as she leaned towards him. Her dress was thin and silky, it was sleeveless and he stroked the firm skin of her arm, following it up her slender neck to her hair.

'Your hair – just the same – so soft and short.' He ruffled it gently. 'Lucky lucky Dave! So you loved him the moment you saw him?'

'I saw him at a cocktail party – at the Graces. Dim lights, a lot of people, a stranger across a crowded terrace – and the world stopped spinning. The way he stood – the way he looked —'

She had taken his hand and put it against the round firm softness of her breast. He felt her heart beating hard and fast.

'I thought it was you,' she said. 'Just for an instant I thought he was you. So I loved him, that was why I loved him. Don't you understand? For a moment I believed you'd come back.'

Her arms encircled his waist as he sat up and she pressed her face against his hard young chest.

'Phil, what are you saying?'

'I'm saying that I love you, my darling. I came with Dave – but I came to you.'

'You came to me – knowing I might be blinded. In pity?'

'In love. It took that terrible calamity to make me know myself. I'll never forget that call from Cape Town on Christmas night. I had only one thought – to get to you. Nothing else mattered. There are no strings, no compromises. If you still want me I'll go with you anywhere in the world.'

'Phil . . . if I want you! I've never stopped wanting you. It's been an ache inside me worse than any pain I've suffered here. Except, perhaps, the fear of being blinded. That was the worst of all because it would kill the last hope that somehow someday I might still have a chance of making you love me.'

'I was the one who was blind,' she said.

'But Dave? Dave was in love with you?'

'Dave was lonely. We were two people who had much in common. We'd both failed in the big adventure of loving. He'd been let down, and I had let you down. We weren't very proud of ourselves. And to me he was a constant reminder of you. If it hadn't been for Dave I might never have got wise to myself. I might have missed the greatest thing in life. I don't think I'm explaining myself very well.'

'Too well,' he said. 'I'm frantically jealous.'

'Don't be. It's nearly a year since you and I said goodbye. That's a long time. I expect I've got someone to be jealous of too. Come on, now, admit it!'

His mouth was against her hair, tender, half smiling as he thought of young Hortense with her straight corn coloured hair and her skin like a Cape peach.

'I was lonely too,' he said. 'There was a girl on a farm near Golden Grass . . . she was very sweet. But there was nothing to it.'

Phil saw again the canyon in the crescent of the rocky Hamersley mountains, a tall pale gum tree, a clear spring gushing, cold as ice, from the warm red rock, and she heard Dave's words, 'We are two lonely people in a lonely place . . .'

'I understand,' she said. 'It was a bit the same for both of us – you and me. But it wasn't real. Only this is good and true – you and me. This girl – will she be there when we go to Golden Grass together?'

'She was only visiting her sister. She'll be gone when we go to Golden Grass together. Did you say that, Phil? When we go to Golden Grass together . . .'

'I said that.'

'You haven't seen it.'

'I'll be happy there.'

'How can you be sure?'

'We'll be together.'

He cupped her face in his hands and his fingertips read her features and the smooth contours of youth as if they were Braille. Straight blunt nose – there'd be freckles across its bridge – arched brows, the left a little higher than the right, soft mobile lips slightly parted, long clean curve of chin and neck and throat.

'I can see you,' he said. 'Never mind the bandages. I'll always see you as you are now. Mine.'

'Yours,' she said. 'Wherever you may be. For always.'

The bell was ringing down the ward, cutting off conversations, parting families and friends.

'I can't let you go,' he said.

'There's tomorrow and the day after and for ever —'

'What will your parents say?'

'They know. I told them before I left. The ward is quiet. Everyone has gone. Goodbye, Franz.'

'Goodbye, Phil. Till tomorrow.'

He heard her step, quick now and lonely on the polished boards, and then the doors closed behind her and everything was very still. He lay back in the darkness and silence but he saw her and heard the echo of her voice and knew that this time he had not been dreaming.